Nich

NEVER DEFEATED: THE FRIGATE

CONSTITUTION

To Jane & Phil
with Love
from the author
N. Orloff

AKVY*PRESS

ISBN 978-0-9877785-3-6
Library of Congress Control Number: 2012935144

Published by AKVY Press:
Coral Springs, Florida, USA; Toronto, Canada

1.Constitution (Frigate) - Historical Fiction. 2. United States - Historical Fiction. 3. Nautical - Fiction. 4.Historical Figures - Fiction. 5.Fiction - Adventure, Adventures & Heroes.

Annotation: The War of 1812 breaks out. The Yankee freedom is at stake. Live free or die decide the frigate Constitution's crew led by Captain Hull. Without given orders they dare to challenge an English frigate. In a severe battle she surrenders to Yankee courage and seamanship. While turning over the pages, you will share the hard life of American sailors and breathe the sea-air. A mosaic of real people and their lives in the whirlpool of War will open to your eyes: the black boy, sacrificing his chance to escape to save his dying white friend, an incredible Captain Hull's love-story as we all only dream of, seamen working above human limits and not giving the Constitution up to the British squadron... You will feel as proud as the ones who fought for the American freedom...

Cover design, cover picture and illustrations:
By the author Nicholas Orloff

AUTHOR'S NOTE

Dear Reader,

Two hundred years ago our country was in peril: foreign troops invaded our land. Washington, D.C., was captured and burnt. The American forces surrendered Fort Dearborn (modern Chicago) and Detroit...
This book is about the heroes who saved our country - the frigate Constitution was the first one to challenge the powerful enemy at sea.

The numerous books, archives, two hundred year-old newspapers, the USS and the British Navy documents, even cemeteries records, are just a small part of what I shoveled up, working on this novel.

This book is a work of fiction. Still, you will be surprised, that practically all the stories or scenes descriptions are actually based on the real events.

- The black boy, James Frances, sacrificing his chance to escape from the British prison "Jersey" in Brooklyn to save his dying white friend;

- An incredible Captain's Hull love-story as we all only dream of;

- The Constitution's race with His Majesty's Ship Santa Margareta;

- The tales of Captain Orne's and Elijah Adams's – the Yankees captured by the British frigate Guerrirere;

While turning over the pages, you will share the hard life of American sailors and breathe the sea-air. As Massachusetts folks in 1812, you will be terrified that at any minute the British might put your village on fire. You will be among those who walked all the way to Boston to greet the Constitution after her great victory.

My wish and hope is that you will feel as proud as the ones who fought for the American freedom...

Nicholas Orloff

ACKNOWLEDGMENTS

I am indebted to the following people for their contributions to this book:

To my family for their love and support.

To my sister, Irene Orloff, for the book editing.

To my friends and history scholars, Burleigh Hickman and Matt Goin, for discussing the events of War 1812, helping with a plot and the book editing.

To my daughter, Tanya Rozova and my daughter in law Juliya Shoshiyeva, for the text editing.

To my publisher, Yuri K. Shestopalov from AKVY Press, for his guidance and support.

To Michael Rozov, a world history expert, my best friend and advisor.

To all of you, from the bottom of my heart, thank you.

♣ ♣ ♣

CHAPTER 1

JULY 1777. BROOKLYN. THE PRISON SHIP "JERSEY". THE PRICE OF LIBERTY

Burning July sun heated the old ship, turning its hold into an oven. In need of some breathable air, the prisoners crowded onto the ladder leading up, even though it was strictly forbidden - the British were scared of mutiny.

A guard in red uniform furiously took a step in, his bayonet set high, ready to thrust. "Stay back from the hatchway, ye Yankee rascals!" he barked, revealing missing teeth, his horse-face purple with anger.

Startled, the men hurried down. Missing their steps, the prisoners landed at the bottom of the ladder, forming a dirty moving heap.

One by one, they struggled out and crawled on all fours like cockroaches into the semi-darkness of the hold. Just one of them, keeping three feet from the ladder, dared to beg "Sir, just a drop of water, Sir, you won't refuse it for my dying brother?"

"Ye, gasbag, stay away! No water today!" Outrage flashed across the horse guard's face. "Ye wanted ye'r Yankee freedom? Get it now!"

The sentry lifted his bayonet again to show the prisoners their place, but the stench stopped him. Pressing his nostrils tight, the guard retired, deciding that disease and the stinky air would do the job and kill the stubborn Yankees soon anyway.

One of the prisoners, James Frances, a black boy whose bones poked through his taut skin, waited until the sound of the guard's feet died. Then he crept to his friend lying motionless in the far corner of the hold. Only ten feet separated the boys, but it was still hard to reach him: the prison was tightly packed with captured Yankees lying on a sticky, filthy floor that had not been swept for years. Trying not to step on anybody's limbs, James passed between a scrawny, long-bearded, dirty man, mumbling a prayer and an ill-looking prisoner pissing into a bucket. The smell almost made the boy pass out. Fighting dizziness, James composed himself to continue on his rough way.

The prison was hell itself. Foul air, scarce stinking food, and scanty putrid water - some days no water at all- murdered fifteen to twenty people every day. Lying among those who were still alive, the departed were waiting for that special hour when, at last, their bodies would be thrown off into the mass grave close by. No wonder that local folks called the old hulk "Hell-ship", long having forgotten its official name "Jersey".

Exhausted, with his heart pounding and head spinning, James reached his friend, Daniel Lewis, and looked at his colorless face with closed eyes. Life was leaking out of the white boy's body. Just eleven years old and already dying... Only two months had passed, since Daniel, the wounded powder-boy, was thrown into the hold, and now it was hardly possible to recognize him. Even Daniel's ugly scar, which ran diagonally thru his forehead as a memory of the battle when a Yankee brig was taken by a British frigate, faded, blended into his pale skin.

James lifted his head and looked around to make sure the guard had not returned. Disgust came to the black boy's face when he noticed a rat feasting on the nose of the lifeless man lying next to his white friend. James jerked his arm to scare the rat off. The obnoxious animal showed its sharp teeth in reply. Then it slowly moved a little just to continue to lunch on the dead man's fingers... In fact, human flesh was the only food available for the armadas of rats on the ship. Barely living Yankee prisoners stopped rat-watching long ago - the rodents were too fast for them to catch anyway.

The Powder-boy himself, James Frances, was captured more than six months ago. He had not seen the sun ever since. How could he survive for so long down in this hell? Had African ancestors passed him a slave-ship surviving gene? God only knows the answer.

The black boy shook his white friend's shoulder and whispered "Dan, can you hear me? Lieutenant Hull, the officer next to me, was exchanged. He will be released today. He told me to hide in his trunk to escape. I say - take my place, mate."

Fighting unconsciousness, Daniel opened his eyes trying to collect his mind.

"Wake up, Dan! You should go instead... It is your last chance," the black friend was saying, "...Two more days and God will take your soul. I'll hide you in the trunk".

"What about ye, James?" Just a whisper came in reply.

A hint of a smile touched the black boy's lips; white teeth sparkled in the dark.

"God willing, we'll meet again, man."

James lifted his head, and helped Daniel get into a canvas trunk just before the horse-faced guard was back.

"Lieutenant Hull, ye're in bloody luck, ye' been exchanged and free to go. Take ye'r bag!" The guard shouted from the hatchway.

A rawboned man in his thirties looking sixty, wearing what was left of his Yankee Lieutenant uniform, struggled to get up with a convulsive cough. "Sir, let this boy help me carry my trunk, please."

The guard burst out laughing "Oh, ye have that much gold that ye ain't able to carry ye'r trunk ye'rself? Ha-ha." However, noticing that Hull appeared more as a shadow than as a human being, he nodded.

James Frances lifted up the heavy trunk, and started dragging his burden between the prisoners. If anybody had noticed him hiding the white friend in the bag, nobody cared to say a word.

Lieutenant Joseph Hull, sick with the fever or was it the beginning of tuberculosis? could hardly stay on his feet. Nevertheless, he pulled the trunk to help the boy. Sweat ran on their faces, hearts hammering loudly, blood whooshed thru their ears covering their gasps for air. Still, Hull and the black boy kept on going. An obstacle stood on their way - the ladder to go up from the hold. How on Earth would they make their way up?

James's heart was about to jump out of his chest but he tried to encourage himself "Pull the trunk, pull it!"

Blood rose to his head, hurting the temples. Three more steps! Could he make it? Where to get the strength?

"Come on, James, one more push. Hold on, Dan, my dear friend!" The black boy was whispering. His lungs burnt inhaling the air thick with the stench of sweat, urine and rotten human flesh.

"James, keep going! Just lift your leg. Pull!" the boy commanded himself stubbornly.

Finally they reached the last step. The bright light blinded them.

In spite of the sharp pain in their eyes, Hull and James could not help looking up to the sky they had been missing for so long. A deep sigh broke from their chests.

They made it!

Lieutenant Hull and James were on the weather deck full of the light of a fair summer day. The black boy's eyes turned red and tears would appear if his tiny body still contained any water – on that hot day no water had been delivered into the prison. Not the first time though...

Knowing the guards were watching, James and the Yankee Lieutenant gathered their last strength and carried their burden to the ship's side.

"Live long, Daniel! God bless you!" James murmured under his breath, not able to turn his eyes off the trunk hiding his little friend.

The British sentinel startled him with his thunderous shout "Ye, black swine, back to the hold!"

Having breathed the fresh air for that short instance, the poor boy had to drag himself back to the dark stuffy hell that had replaced his home for the past six months.

♣ ♣ ♣

CHAPTER 2

July 1810. OPEN SEA. WEST INDIES. NANTUCKET SLEIGH RIDE

After three weeks of dead calm under the scorching equatorial sun, a squall broke out suddenly in the late afternoon. Gale force winds foamed the ocean, coloring it white.

Angry seas carried the old Nantucket whaler "Martha" at their will somewhere south of the Lesser Antilles Islands in the West Indies. In the dusk before sunrise, the gusty wind died, replaced by a soft breeze. All sails set, seamen free of watch, worn-out by a tough night, dropped to catch some sleep before the day chores began.

"Martha", a 105-feet long ship, was heading to the Pacific around Cape Horn. Knowing that there was still a slim chance of seeing a whale in the Atlantic, the seamen kept watch in a crow-nest, a small lookout platform at the top of the ship's mast. None of them could forget the stories of the blessed old times when whales could be found in abundance just off Cape Cod.

With the first shy morning light, John Dickinson, a young strong sailor went up, eagerly wanting to hunt whales. John's fiancée, the beautiful red-haired Marie, was waiting for his fast return so that they could get married and buy a little house of their own. Two months at sea, and every second the young seaman dreamt about holding Marie close to him and listening to her tender voice.

Thinking about the house he would buy upon his return, John saw a whale just three miles from the ship, then another one, and two more further as long shadows in the hazy air. The young seaman rubbed his eyes and took another look wondering was it true or was it the restless night playing tricks with his eyes. What he saw was incredible: a school of whales! In the Atlantic! How could it be?

The sailor's heart began pounding loudly: huge sea animals, the subject of his deepest desire, were there, drifting with the current, leisurely moving their tail flukes.

"Whale ho! There she blows!" John shouted, almost choking with happiness.

"Where away?" The First Mate shrieked from the deck.

"One point on the weather bow!"

"How far?"

"Three miles!"

"Keep your eye on her!"

"Four whales! No, five!"

"Cry out when we head right!" The First Mate took the helm, changing the course.

Clam, the Captain's dog, greeted the news barking joyfully, his tail wagging vigorously. Waking up to the sound of "There she blows", the crew, all twenty one men poured onto the deck eager to find out if they were the right whales – those good for hunting - slow swimmers that kept floating when killed. A harpooned blue fin – the wrong kind- would drag a boat deep under the water. Lots of seamen lost their lives for their greed in daring to catch them.

"Sperm-whales!" The seamen's faces lit up – those were the kind of whales they were praying for.

The command to furl the sails followed and when the ship was less than half a mile away, the Captain ordered to lower the whaling boats. Soon they were racing towards the whales with the ship-captain as the coxswain on one boat and the first and the second mates on the other two. Beside them a harpooner and four rowers were manning each boat.

Seamen tried to get closer to the sea-animals that were periodically blowing or turning their flukes up and sinking, committed to their peaceful breakfast ceremonial.

Rowers and harpooners worked hard with their oars to be at the right place when the mammal would come back to the surface. Coxswains steered, keeping a quarter of a mile distance to another boat.

A huge sixty foot long bull (a male whale) erected just in front of the Captain's boat. In a flash, John's Dickinson uncle, Caleb Smith, – the harpooner – skillfully plunged his two sharp irons each attached to a tow-line into the side of the whale.

"Tomahawk" was Caleb's nickname, not without good reason. This time his keen eye and firm arm did not fail either, hitting the animal's vital spot. The whale spouted a red and pink fountain – water mixing with blood – and then it suddenly ran furiously away, having the Captain's boat in tow – taking the boat for a "Nantucket sleigh ride" as whalers around the world called it. That Massachusetts Island had become a center of the whaling industry. Other Yankee cities and even other countries were eager to get experienced

Nantucket sailors on their ships to learn from the best about hunting the sea beasts.

"Hold-o-o-n," the Captain shouted.

Bending lower and clenching the boat's sides with their white knuckles, the drenched seamen prayed: "God, please don't let it go underwater. Please make it stop."

Being thrown from the boat during a wild ride meant just one thing. Death. Not many whalers could swim and, anyway, it could take a while for their mates to get to the spot. Most likely, too late...

Just young Dickenson dared to laugh, holding tight, – the hunt was bringing him closer to Marie.

The boat raced thru the seas, tossing water spray for half an hour. Then the whale dove down, fortunately making just a shallow submerge. It was up to the Captain, a skilled whale-hunter, to cut the tow-line if he foresaw the whale would dive deeper than the towing line length (six hundred feet) thus pulling the boat under water and bringing death to the sailors. Sometimes even a hat would not come back to the surface - the ocean-deeps swallowed everything.

However, that day all was going fine – the second boat happened to be just next to the spot where the huge animal arose. The first mate poked its fluke lance to sever the whale's tail tendons. Dirty work but someone had to do it: the desperate beast could thrash wildly and smash the boat. With his tail no longer obeying, the animal could neither dive nor swim. In a split second all was over - the whale floated motionless. Ten minutes had not passed as a hawser was fastened around its tail, and the pull started to get the catch alongside the ship.

"Whoo-heee! What a lucky day. A sixty foot long sperm whale! At least a hundred fifty barrels of oil," the seamen in the boats were chuckling. It was the tenth part of the fifteen hundred barrels that the old ship was aiming to get on the cruise. The old fat bull was the biggest sperm whale the sailors had ever seen, on average providing seventy-eighty barrels of oil.

Still a mile and a half from the whaler, the seamen suddenly noticed an English frigate pulling alongside "Martha", moving from behind their ship. Busy hunting, nobody spotted it before.

"Dear Lord!" the sailors started saying their prayers – meeting a British man-of-war did not promise anything good. If the whalers were aboard their ship, they would lower the sails and try to flee letting down their so-hard gotten prey. However, today it was too late – "Martha" could not sail off with just five souls aboard, leaving the others in the sea.

When the whaler-boats reached their ship, the British with their muskets and pistols in hands sat comfortably on the deck with their frigate guns run out of the ports. They were ready to fire.

A British lieutenant, a young man of eighteen, tried to look important addressing the Yankee Captain. "Captain, His Majesty ship "Guerrirere" is in need of jack tars. We will press your sailors. I'll get five!"

The whaler Captain, his heart at his knees, begged "I got just twenty hands, you take five of them and we will not be able to sail any further."

"Are fifteen not enough to clean your nasty deck? Ha-ha. I am just following my orders," said the Lieutenant, his eyes already fixed on the Yankee seamen. "His Majesty needs only the youngest and strongest ones."

He pointed at John Dickinson "That one will do!"

John Dickinson's heart skipped a beat - the Yankees pressed into His Majesty's Navy never return. The British hang from a yardarm those who tried to escape. What would happen to his Marie? What about their house they dreamed of? What about his life, for God's sake?

Taking the last chance, John Dickinson saluted his Captain "I beg your pardon, Sir, but I was born in Nantucket, they can't press me. I have my Seaman Protection Certificate from Boston."

The Lieutenant burst out with laughter. "You look older than twenty five! It means you were born under the King as subject to the British crown!"

The Captain, his face purple and trembling with rage, murmured "But... our Independence... we are different countries now."

"Like I give a damn!" The Lieutenant grinned. "You refuse," he pointed at the frigate guns ready to shoot– "Your ship will sink to the bottom. Show the fish your certificates then!"

As if he understood the threat, Clam – the dog growled at the British, baring its fangs.

The Lieutenant was fast. Taking out his pistol, he aimed at the dog.

"No-o-o-o," the Captain shouted lifting his arm to protect the dog.

Laughing, the Lieutenant pulled the trigger.

The shot cut the calm afternoon.

Clam yelped and dropped to the floor, blood streaming from his wound...

Ten minutes later all was over - the British selected four more men and, with muskets aimed at their backs, led the pressed sailors to their waiting cutter.

"Permission to say farewell?" shouted Caleb Smith to the Lieutenant, and, not waiting for a reply, he jumped to hug his nephew, determination in his eyes.

"Tell Marie I love her! " John Dickinson murmured, smearing tears on Tomahawk's chest, "tell her, I'll do anything to come back! I'll swim if necessary! ...If she could only wait..."

The harpooner nodded not able to say a word – tears suffocated him. Feeling like he was hit by lightning, the Captain stayed beside him motionless.

Gathering his last strength and leaving a red track on the deck floor, Clam crawled toward his master and nuzzled his hand. The old Captain dropped on his knees and looked at the dog's eyes that were saying their final farewell...

The rest of the Yankee crew, fifteen dreary whalers, watched as their mates were taken aboard the frigate.

Soon, the British ship set her sails and raced off, ruining the Martha's voyage, seamen's hopes, and their lives...

♣ ♣ ♣

CHAPTER 3

4th OF JULY 1812. ANNAPOLIS, MARYLAND. VOLUNTEERS

The frigate Constitution was under repair when the war with Great Britain was declared two weeks earlier. And on the 4th of July the ship's Captain, Isaac Hull, hurried to have the Constitution ready to sail even though no orders from the Admiralty had been received yet.

Everything had to be taken care of: water, food-barrels, spare sails, timber, gun-powder, not to mention the crew itself...

The busy noon caught the Captain leaning over the charts spread on the large table in the middle of the Great Cabin.

Besides the table, just two carronades, a long gun, a dresser, and a rack with sea maps were all that the Great Cabin possessed. No stove for heating in winter, no sofa, no rugs, still Hull considered it luxury after his twenty five years at sea.

The Captain went thru all the steps of a seaman's career, starting as a steward at fourteen, becoming Master of a schooner after being ordinary, then an able seaman, afterwards accepting Fourth Lieutenant's duty on the Constitution, when he fell in love with her for the rest of his life. Thirty nine years old Captain felt privileged to command one of the biggest among the eight Yankee frigates.

Hull's work was interrupted by his First Lieutenant, Charles Morris, who had been serving under him since the Barbary War, "Sir, package from the Admiralty!"

The Captain opened the package, unfolded the letter, which said:

"Navy Department
3rd July, 1812

Sir,
As soon as the Constitution is ready for sea, you will weigh anchor and proceed to New York.
...If, on your way thither, you should fall in with an enemy's vessel, you will be guided in your proceeding by your own judgment, bearing in mind, however, that you are not voluntarily to encounter a force superior to your own.
On your arrival at New York, you will report yourself to Commodore Rodgers. If he should not be in that port, you will remain there until further orders.

P. Hamilton"

After reading the first sentence, Hull lifted his head, excitement in his eyes.

"Charles, my orders! To join our squadron in New York on the utmost dispatch."

The Captain's servant Ivan Stone, a thin scarred seaman of about fifty, opened the door ajar and coughed politely. "Sir, Mr. Purser and the Master to see you!"

The Purser - Mr. Chew and the Sailing Master- Mr. Alwyn stepped into the cabin saluting the Captain.

"Sir, full compliment at last! Our luck, many prime seamen in today's draft! Though, most are whalers and merchants, never served in the Navy," reported sailing master Alwyn in a quick, military manner.

"They'll learn! Very good, thank you, Mr. Alwyn," said Captain and then he questioned Mr. Chew, "Mr. Purser, the gun powder?"

"Just finished loading. Food barrels are in!"

"Good job, Mr. Chew!"

"Sir, four more seamen- volunteers just came, I told them the frigate was completely manned, still they insist you know them and beg to pass you their names," said the sailing master.

"Who are they?"

Alwyn checked a small piece of paper "Daniel Lewis, James Frances, Caleb Smith, and Squeaking John. All are salt."

"Squeaking John... Daniel Lewis... Get them in at once!"

Alwyn opened the door "Stone, get the volunteers in!"

Foreseeing the order, Ivan Stone immediately reappeared with four sailors in their late forties. The newcomers took their hats off and greeted the Captain touching their foreheads with bent fingers.

Hull's attention was caught by the disfigured face of Seaman Lewis. Recollecting something, Hull smiled widely "Bah, Daniel, I would recognize this scar anywhere!"

Daniel Lewis nodded and said politely "Aye, Sir, aye, it's I." Then, pointing at a black sailor "And, sir, if ye please, this man James Frances saved my life hiding me in ye'r father's trunk in Brooklyn prison years ago."

"An honor to meet you, James! Your bravery was a legend in my family!" Hull shook the black sailor's hand – an unusual gesture – no captain shook hands with common seamen.

White teeth sparkled in a broad smile on the shining face. "Aye, aye, Sir!"

Turning to Squeaking John, Hull tapped the sailor on his shoulder "Squeaking John, old chap! I trust I find you well?"

The seaman reported in a formal, squeaking voice. "Sir, able seamen Caleb Smith and Squeaking John volunteer on frigate Constitution!"

"But you have got to be fifty by now!"

"Sir, as soon as we heard Captain Hull's in need of jack tars, we walked all the way from Philly!"

Hull smiled. "Squeaking John, are your eyes as keen as they used to be?"

"Almost so, aye-aye, Sir! They're all right to aim at the enemy!"

"And where is your nephew, Caleb?" the Captain asked.

"Two years back pressed from a whaler, Sir. Never heard from him since," reported Caleb, nicknamed "the Tomahawk".

"Bastards!" Hull clutched his fists. Then he turned to his purser. "Mr. Chew, I'd like to take these men! Rate them as able seamen!"

The purser saluted "Yes, sir!" and gestured to the seaman "This way. Follow me."

The volunteers touched their foreheads with bent fingers and went out of the Great Cabin lead by the Purser and the Master.

Hull shook his head in disbelief, smiling, "Daniel Lewis – he was a kid when my father brought him into our Connecticut house. I was six then and could not stop thinking about the brave black teen, sacrificing his chance to escape!" said the Captain to his First Lieutenant.

The glimpses of his uneasy childhood came to Hull's mind... The fear entirely consuming his family in a small Connecticut town when the boy's father was in the British prison. The never-stopping dread when his father returned, coughing blood, and the local doctor said no remedy could be found. The orphanage, then adoption by his uncle, General William Hull. The only pleasant souvenir of his childhood was the trip with his father, captain of a merchant-ship to West Indies, when the boy forever fell in love with the sea.

As if waking up, Hull added "Squeaking John and Caleb Smith taught me my first sea-knots on a merchant. Then John sailed with me in the Barbary War! Skilled gunner and a brave heart!"

Still smiling, Hull winked to Morris "Besides, Squeaking John brings luck!"

"How so, Sir?"

"Later! One day I'll tell you. No time to lose now," said Hull, and continued formally "Mr. Morris, muster the crew at 4 pm! And Mr. Morris, pass the word to all officers to ease up on new hands until they learn their stations and duties!"

"Aye-aye, sir!"

The First Lieutenant saluted Hull and hustled out of the Great Cabin.

♣ ♣ ♣

CHAPTER 4

4th OF JULY 1812. ANNAPOLIS, MARYLAND.
MUSTERING FOR DEVISIONS

By the time the Constitution bell tolled eight – 4 pm, the frigate crew, four hundred and fifty souls, were on the upper –spar- deck filling gangways, forecastle and quarterdeck mustered for divisions. Everybody, washed and shaved; all attention to their Captain on the quarterdeck.

Golden epaulets, yellow metal buttons with an anchor and American eagle surrounded with fifteen stars, shone on Hull's blue coat reflecting the afternoon sun. Beside the Captain, also in their best uniforms, stood First and Second Lieutenants Charles Morris and Alexander Wardsworth, George Read as the Third and Beckman Hoffman as Fourth Lieutenants and Acting Lieutenant John Shubrick.

The sailing master Alwyn commanded "Toe the line!"

Sailors executed willingly, so did the four new able seaman-volunteers on the forecastle eager to catch each of their Captain's words.

"Constitutions! Today is the 4th of July! It's been thirty six years since we got our freedom! Still, the British refuse to accept it: they capture our merchants and whalers. They press our ships to man their Navy! The British pressing gangs dare catch men on our shores. On the very streets of Boston!"

A murmur of anger started among the crew. Morris jerked to stop the noise but after recalling Captain's order, he gave in.

"We are for sailors' rights!" continued Hull.

Sailors echoed "Aye, sailors' rights!"

"Shipmates! Our country has just eight frigates against the British thousand... To win this war, we have to surpass the English in ship handling and gunnery. They are fighting JUST FOR PAY and we are fighting for OUR NATION! We are fighting TO LIVE FREE OR DIE!"

A loud explosion of agreeable shouts escaped the sailors' chests. Seaman James Ashford closed his eyes and repeated slowly the Captain's words as if apprehending their sense "...live free or die!"

Hull, his face sobering without a hint of a smile, took a long look at his crew, then resumed his speech.

"Constitutions! Tomorrow we'll sail to New York to join the squadron. Though we will get to New York before the Brits come down from their blockading station in Halifax no time to waste! Starting tomorrow all of us will be having a hard time, I repeat, VERY HARD. We will learn to work the ship with new hands. Gun exercise is to be held every day. Are you all ready to do your duty?"

The gangways, the forecastle and quarterdeck answered as one man "Ready! HUZZAH! For our nation!"

Freedom is blessed: it gave Yankee seamen the strength to fight the greatest empire of all time. In the year 1812 thirteen million square miles of land belonged to the British crown, spread over five continents. The Royal Navy guns, the English pride, held the enormous empire together. Two hundred ninety six frigates, not to mention three hundred ships-of-the-line, also called two-deckers, with more than sixty long guns each. That armada could force any country to the knees but not the young United States that dared to declare their independence. Just eight frigates and no ships-of-the line, it was all the young country had against the greatest power with thirty years of sea-battle traditions...

♣ ♣ ♣

CHAPTER 5

4th OF JULY 1812. ANNAPOLIS, MARYLAND.
BERTH-DECK

The 4th of July grog was drunk and the carronades salute died away replaced by seamen's regular non-stop work around the ship with just two hours break in the evening. Still the starboard watch had an hour left before going to their stations. Enjoying every minute of it, the sailors sat talking around a long table lit by a hanging lamp, forgetting about the humid stuffy air that made them sweat.

Old Constitution seaman John Brown took a place next to the table, listening to the conversation while looking at himself in a small dim mirror and applying tar to his long hair, the subject of his pride. Suddenly John caught a reflection of a rawboned boy aged twelve or thirteen, who long ago overgrew his clothes, staring at him, surprise on his face.

The old sailor twisted his head around. Recognizing the new powder-boy from today's draft, Brown winked "Ahoy, kid, got a name?"

"Peter Furnace, Sir!" the boy lifted his head and straightened his back eager to look taller. "Can ye tell kindly why do ye tar ye hair?"

"Ain't ye know why they call sailors "Jack Tar"? If ye are aloft making sail and ye hair ai't caught in the rigging, ye're a dead-monkey hanging head-down. Ha-ha.. Come, Peter, I'll do ye hair. "

Smiling, Peter took a seat on the floor in front of the sailor. Having opened the sea-chest with letters "John Brown" on its lid, the old seaman took out a bone comb and a small blue ribbon. After combing Peter's long curls, he tied a pony tail with the ribbon. Then John slightly smeared the boy's hair with tar.

"Got a family, Peter?"

"Mother and two youngsters, Sir! Mother's sick."

"And ye father, my lad?"

"I ain't got no father. Killed on 'Chesapeake'."

"In year seven, says I? When the English two-decker Leopard shot at our Chesapeake?"

"Yea... Three kids to feed... Ain't no husband to support. Mother broke her backbone carrying coal and water for rich folks..." The boy's voice trembled, he snuffled, and tears showed in his eyes. Turning away, Peter wiped them with his sleeve.

As soon as the sailors heard the word "Leopard", all conversations at the table stopped, everybody turned their heads. Five years passed, still the 56-gun Leopard firing without a warning at a US war-ship just off the Virginia coast hurt every Yankee soul.

"Dey bloody "Leopard" wanted to press our frigate!" a young seaman Hogan cried out, his face a color of beets.

"What say ye? They killed and wounded twenny 'Chesapeake' men along with the Captain!" Squeaking John continued.

"In peace time, I says!" Seaman Lewis's ugly scar got red with anger.

"They bloody lubbers hanged five British sailors with Yankee papers. What for, ye say? Hell and fire to them!" Seaman James Cheever joined, his eyes glinting.

"D'ye see, mates, Captain's right. We have to shoot better than those bloody English to defend ourselves! D'ye hear me?" Asa Curtis shouted.

"Hear him! Hear him," Other sailors cried out loud.

Their shouts were interrupted by the ship's bell tolling 8 pm. The last sound had not have died away yet as boatswain Robert Adams, an old hefty sailor with a saber scar across his weather-beaten cheek, came down the berth deck.

"First night watch! To your stations!"

The boatswain did not need to say it twice - seamen rushed to a ladder leading up. Their mates from the previous Second Dog watch took their place in the berth deck. Adams' pipe had not finished "Hammocks down" signal as, immediately, not a moment wasted, sailors hung their hammocks. In a minute only the sound of sleeping men was heard.

One sailor began snoring; another one joined piping loud, both sounding in unison with other men murmuring, under the accompaniment of ship noise and thunderous farts – the holiday treat – a dish of beans with fresh pork, a real feast in seamen's opinion, was to be blamed. Nothing could wake them up tired as they were.

Customarily at sea each watch had no more than four hours to sleep. Four hours unless "All hands round the ship" was heard during the night, calling all to set sails.

Boatswain Adams took the lantern and went up the stairs leaving the berth in the dark.

♣ ♣ ♣

CHAPTER 6

4th OF JULY 1812. ANNAPOLIS, MARYLAND. ANN HART

That night, taking an advantage of the last couple of hours at the harbor, the Captain Hull hurried to write a letter to mail it before sailing off.

"My Dear brother,

Your letter was a pleasant surprise! I am overjoyed to know your wife and kids are doing fine. God Bless them!
Sorry, I did not reply sooner. I was extremely occupied getting the Constitution ready. After my cruise to Europe half of the crew had to be replaced, their contracts being expired. However, I am lucky – lots of prime seamen volunteered. Many are merchants or whalers thus they are skilled at making sails. However, they need to start 'feeling' the Constitution. She is a stout and fast sailor, I dearly love her."

Captain's servant, Ivan Stone, peaked into the door and coughed politely.
"Anything else, Captain?"
"No, thankee. Go to sleep, Ivan. Heaving anchor at four bells," said Hull, for a landsman that would mean 2 am.

Ivan retired, shuffling his rheumatic feet, and Hull came back to his letter.

"You ask me again whether I am planning to get married. The answer is no, not yet, although I wish... You know I didn't have time to look for a bride. Thirty nine year old now, I am still waiting for my soul mate. And who would wait for a husband who is always at sea?"

As if answering his question, a young girl's voice sounded in his mind "I will wait. I will always keep him in my heart, and he will find his way home!"

Hull's pen stopped. His mind drifted in memories ten years back. A soft smile touched his lips...

Summer of 1802. Noise of the busy Boston dock filled the air as the Constitution was getting repaired after the Quasi War with France. A carpenter and his mates in working clothes were rigging the frigate. A very young Lieutenant Hull kept an eye on the whole scene, very proud of being in charge of all the work. His bright blue eyes sparkled with energy and enthusiasm.

"Mr. Johns, repairs on this block will not do. We should replace it, should we not, Mr. Johns?" Hull asked the carpenter.

"You are right, sir, sorry I missed it. Will fix right away. Give me a hand, lads!"

Two carpenter's mates rushed to execute the order. A midshipman, a sixteen year old boy, saluted Hull.

"Beg your pardon, Sir, a group of school girls ask to see you. I believe you were expecting them, weren't you?"

"Oh, God, don't have time for that!" said Hull to himself, then addressing the midshipman, "Mr. Gross, let the young ladies on the deck."

A group of girls aged twelve-fourteen stepped on the Constitution spar-deck, all excited and solemn. The midshipman was leading the way, a broad smile on his face.

Leaving his work, Hull walked to the starboard bow to meet the visitors "Good afternoon, ladies! Welcome aboard the Constitution! First Lieutenant, Hull, at your service."

Girls curtsied and looked at him with awe, then greeted the Lieutenant all at the same time "Good afternoon, Mr. Hull!"

One girl, hiding behind her school-mates, whispered "What a dashing lieutenant!"

"Seen his eyes? Pure blue! And his sun-tanned face makes them even deeper!" The second girl giggled.

"How stout he is! What a handsome man!" The first one could not stop but saying.

"What lovely chestnut curly hair," the third one chirped.

Their schoolmate, a girl with red freckles on her round face curtsied "Sir, would you please show us the ship?"

"My pleasure! You are currently on the spar-deck also called the weather deck. The forward part of the weather deck is the forecastle. Behind us is the quarterdeck. Here you can see the helm and binnacles. Three masts: fore, main and mizzen," pointed Hull with his finger, then he added proudly, "The main mast is two hundred twenty feet from the keel to the truck!"

"Oh, really? Excuse me, Sir, does this mean seamen have to climb up that high to make sails?" The same red freckled girl was wondering.

"Yes, they do!" Hull answered, slightly amazed: after twenty five years at sea it became so obvious to him, though it could surprise a landsman.

"Mr. Hull, isn't it dangerous?" A second girl with a green ribbon in her hair asked, narrowing her eyes.

"Sometimes it is, especially in the high seas. Being a seaman is not easy, you know," Hull said, then noticing how a gloom dropped on the girls' faces, paused and tried to lighten up their mood "...for one thing - you have to tar your hair!"

Hull smiled. The girls giggled and followed him further.

"Here, on spar-deck we have twenty two carronades. Can you imagine them firing 32-pound iron balls!"

School girls didn't show much enthusiasm in this specific subject matter and thus they wandered down onto the gun deck.

"This is our gun deck. It is where we have thirty long guns. Carronades are good for a very short distance however this specific one can throw a twenty four-pound ball for almost a thousand yards!" Hull said boastfully.

"Mr. Hull, is there much noise when a gun is fired?" The first girl with freckles inquired.

The Lieutenant smiled "You know, battle around, you don't care much about the noise." Then wishing to change the subject, he added "Oh, by the way, it's our galley-stove, here, in the middle of the gun-deck. This side of the stove with those large containers is for the seamen. Another side of the galley is for the officers."

"Mr.Hull, what do the crew eat?" The green ribbon girl asked.

"For breakfast seamen have tea and usually oatmeal. For dinner salted meat with beans or dry pies. The crew's favorite days are Sundays and Thursdays, it is when the cook makes Plum Duff."

It looked like this subject was more attractive to the girls than the ship's carronades.

"Mr. Hull, what is "Plum Duff"? Some kind of pudding, isn't it? Must be something good." The girl with red freckles wondered.

"It is flour boiled in water with a bit of salt and sugar."

The girls grimaced - the recipe obviously did not inspire them.

"What about supper?" The Green Ribbon could not stop.

"Ship's biscuits with water. And some grog."

"Fee" The girls were discouraged with the frigate's rations.

"My father, the Mayor," The Red Freckled girl paused to let the importance of her words to be absorbed, "...told me that you surely, have plenty of fish from the sea!"

Hull's response was a big disappointment for Mayor's daughter. "Unfortunately, ship-of-war sailors don't have time for fishing. They are busy with work all the time."

"Sir, I wonder how it could be. I heard s ship might sail for weeks, even months without touching the shore. You must have plenty of time!" The Green Ribbon said with a confidence.

"Oh, no, the crew is busy trimming, furling, making sails. Besides, all the guns should be checked, and repaired. Just in the evening sailors have two hours for themselves. It's when they fix their clothes, cut hair, shave or sing on the forecastle if the weather permits."

"Mr. Hull, do you have a stove in each cabin?" The Red Freckles girl's curiosity had not been satisfied yet.

"No, it's the only stove on the ship."

"How then do you warm the rooms where people sleep?" It was The Red Freckles again.

"No, we don't warm either the officers' cabins or the berth deck," Hull said abruptly, trying to finish such questions.

"What about winter?"

"Even in winter. You know, it is dangerous to have stoves on a ship. Besides, when you are at sea, how much firewood could a frigate carry?"

"But it must be very cold then."

"Seamen's bodies get used to it," said Hull firmly and hurried to change the subject. "Let's go downstairs. Below the gun deck there is the berth-deck."

When they stepped down the ladder, he pointed to the large room at the stern of the ship. "This is our ward-room where the officers have their meals and gather when they are off watch. See those doors? Behind them First, Second Lieutenant's, Lieutenant of Marines, and other officer's cabins".

"If we go fore, you will find where seamen hang their hammocks, fourteen-inches for each. In this berth two hundred hammocks are hanged nightly."

"Just fourteen inches? And where do the other two hundred seamen sleep then?" The third girl in a red dress wondered, surprise on her face.

"In here. Each watch has exactly four hours to sleep. They switch."

"Just four hours? Every day and just four hours? How can it be?" The Red Freckles exclaimed in disbelief.

"You know, men get used to it. No matter how tired sailors are, they fall fast asleep once in their hammocks. Nobody says sea-life is easy. But if you fall in love with the sea..."

Hull stopped abruptly and led them up to the sunny spar deck.

A girl of eleven or twelve year old, named Ann Hart, was watching the Lieutenant with her huge wide–open eyes. So far, she had not said a word. "The deck smells so nice, Sir!"

Hull looked at her and smiled. "You are right; it is the smell of tar mixed with timber and sea air. I love this smell myself. The most wonderful smell in the world!"

"Fee, what a perfume! Ha-ha" The freckled girl giggled.

Other girls chuckled too. Ann Hart didn't. She was looking up at the rigging, dream in her eyes. "I wish I could be a sailor myself! Or at least my husband could!"

"Then you will be waiting for your husband for years not sure he will ever be back!" The red dress said.

"I will wait. I will always keep him in my heart, and he will find his way home!" Ann answered as if coming from her dream.

The girls giggled even louder. Hull, however, was stunned to hear those words from such a young girl.

Nevertheless, the visit was over. The girls chirped "Good bye, Mr. Hull. Thank you for showing us around."

"Good bye, Ladies," saluted Hull.

Ann hesitated for a minute then asked, "Mr. Hull, may I take something from the Constitution to remind me of this visit?"

Smiling, Hull looked at her "I regret, Lady, all you see here is US Navy property, not mine."

Suddenly a small piece of rope on the deck caught his eye. He lifted it up, and in no time tied sea-knots, skillfully making a stunning ornament before handing it to Ann. She eagerly took the souvenir.

"Looks so lovely! And the same nice smell! Thank you, Mr. Hull, I will treasure it for all my life."

"What is your name, young Lady?" Hull asked.

"Ann McCurdy Hart, Sir! I am from Say Brook, Connecticut."

"Oh, really? I am from Connecticut myself, from Derby not so far from Say Brook. It was so nice to meet you, Miss Hart. God bless you!"

Ann hurried to join her school-mates waiting for her on the shore, proudly wearing the rope circle as a necklace. At the sight of her rope-necklace, the girls burst out laughing.

"A rope necklace, you silly thing! Ha-ha!"

Ann didn't seem to care. She turned her head and met Hull's eyes still watching her, deep in amazement. Forgetting about everything else, feeling there were just two of them in the whole world, the Lieutenant and Ann were looking at each other for a while. Neither of them had that feeling before...

As if waking up, Hull smiled, lifted his hand, waved to her, and returned to his duty...

Back from his thoughts, Hull said to himself "I wonder where that Ann-girl is. She should be twenty two by now and probably a good wife for a lucky sailor. God be with her! When I feel lonely, the memory of that girl warms my heart!"

The Captain stood up and walked to the stern window.

It seemed that the calm sea was caressing the Constitution, slowly lifting her up and down. Still thinking about Ann and smiling quietly, Hull gazed at the silver moon reflection running far as a sparkling path on the dark water-surface.

"I hope, one day..." The Captain's did not finish his thought as the ship's bell on the spar-deck above his head stroked two: 9 pm. Hull came back to the table, looked at his letter, and wrote to finish:

"Tomorrow we are sailing to New York. If it's God's will, I hope to meet you there. God bless you and keep your family safe in these difficult times of war,

Your brother Isaac
Annapolis, Maryland
4th of July of year 1812."

After putting the letter into an envelope, the Captain took the lamp and headed first to a small gallery with windows at the side of the ship, where a toilet was made in a wooden bench opening directly into the sea. What a luxury! All others had to go to the head of the ship where five toilet-boxes were placed. Strong wind, storm, rain, snow and sea-waves soaking you wet - still you had to go to the head taking care not to slip overboard, and take your pants down. Fortunately, the sailors were not in the need to use it often as landsmen do. Hard labor made seamen stomachs burn down all nutrition from the scarce ship food and drinking-water, also limited. If diarrhea happened, and how could it be otherwise on a long cruise when drinking water got foul, that was another story though. Grog (rum mixed with three parts of water) was an absolute necessity killing the germs in seamen's stomachs. Besides, it was the joy of the ship's crew.

After using the toilet, Hull glanced thru the gallery windows at his ship's dark masts with bended sails. He knew that he could completely rely on Sailing Master Alwyn and his First Lieutenant. Still it was his captain's habit to be aware of what was going on the ship. Making sure that everything looked right and ready to the sea, Hull headed to his tiny sleeping cabin with a small cot and a little dresser.

He poured just a glass of precious fresh water into a small basin on a dresser from the water-vessel hanging above. At sea they washed their faces and clothes with sea-water. What a treat to feel fresh-water on your face! Having washed his face, he let it dry out by itself, then wiped his hands with a towel. Once undressed and stretched on his cot, the Captain, cradled by the sea, fell fast asleep.

In three hours he had to heave anchor, and leave the Annapolis harbor.

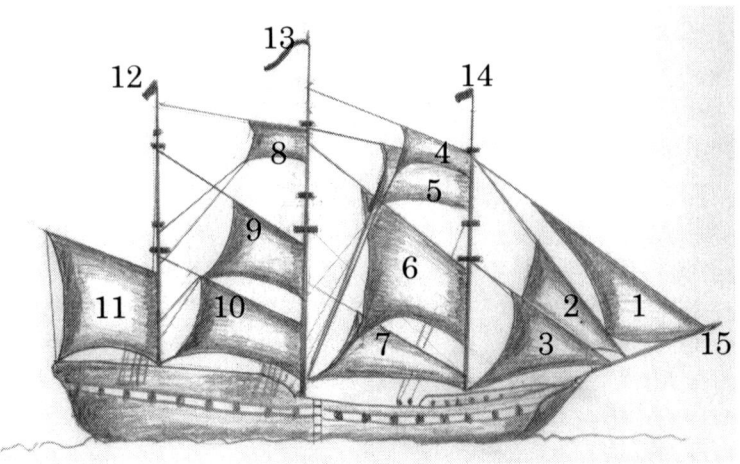

Fore-And-Aft Sails:
1. Jib
2. Fore topmast staysail
3. Fore staysail
4. Main topgallant staysail
5. Middle staysail
6. Main topmast staysail
7. Main staysail
8. Mizzen topgallant staysail
9. Mizzen topmast staysail
10. Mizzen staysail
11. Spanker

Masts:
12. Mizzen
13. Main mast
14. Fore mast
15. Bowsprit

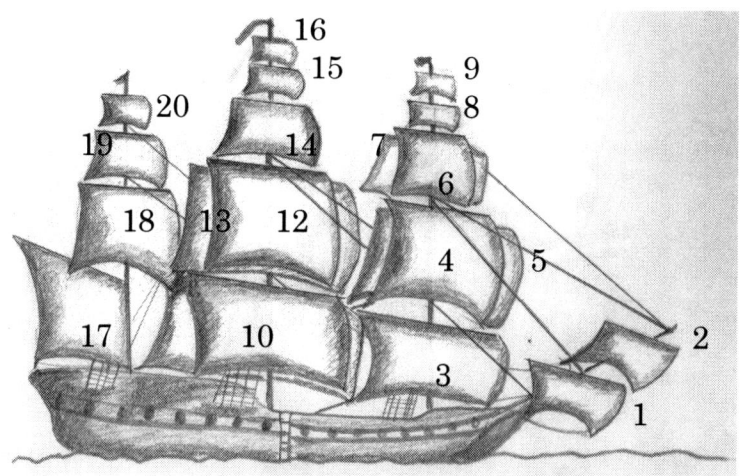

The Square Sails

1. Spritsail course
2. Spritsail topsail
3. Fore course
4. Fore topsail
5. Fore topmast studding sails
6. Fore topgallant sail
7. Fore topgallant studding sails
8. Fore royal
9. Fore sky sail
10. Main course
11. Main studding sails
12. Main topsail
13. Main topmast studding sails
14. Main topgallant sail
15. Main royal
16. Main sky sail
17. Spanker
18. Mizzen topsail
19. Mizzen topgallant
20. Mizzen royal

♣ ♣ ♣

CHAPTER 7

5th OF JULY 1812. MARYLAND COAST WATERS. THE FIRST DAY AT SEA

The ship was in the open sea working under a light breeze at the break of the day when the boatswain Adams' pipes sounded.

"Reveille! Reveille! Give the ship a clean sweep down fore and aft! Rise and shine sleepy heads! Hammocks up! All hands ahoy! Show a leg there!"

Sailors first jumped out of their hammocks, and then were waking up. They ran, getting dressed on the way and bundling their hammocks at the same time before putting them into the netting on the spar deck. No complaints heard.

Peter Furnace, a new powder boy, unsteady on his feet and pale from sea-sickness, ran along with the sailors. Like the others, he put his hammock into the netting.

"John Brown, why do we put hammocks in the netting? If the rain comes, the hammocks will go wet, ain't them?"

The old seaman smiled "When an enemy fires, it's better to get an oak splinter in ye'r hammock than in ye'r guts!" and headed away, followed by the boy.

Stopping suddenly, Peter covered his mouth with both hands, and rushed to the ship's head to throw up. Missing the toilet box, he spewed yesterday's dinner all over the ship's head. It looked like the boy was not the only one who did not feel well on the first day at sea. The floor was covered with filth of landsmen vomiting.

That day the old seamen John Brown and twenty years younger James Cheever, were assigned the duty to clean up the head of the ship. Having a bucket with a rope to catch water in one hand and a holy-stone in the other, both sailors approached the duty spot. A disgusted sigh broke out of their chests.

"Yuckyyyy" James Cheever said pointing at the filth.

"Landsmen, what would ye expect," John Brown nodded.

Both looked at their bare and still clean feet. Shoes were too expensive to wear every day. Exceptions were made only on special occasions as mustering for divisions.

Trying his luck, the younger seaman jabbed an elbow in his mate's side "Hey, look, you can go first - ye'r feet are dirtier than mine!"

John Brown giggled "Sure, I am older!"

Both sailors cracked out laughing as the small trick did not succeed, and then both went over the rope-railing separating the spar deck and the ship's head. After numerous buckets of sea-water were poured on the toilet-boxes and the floor-planks, scrubbing and holy-stoning went on until the work was done.

Once they finished, the seamen looked around. Smiling, James Cheever said "Clean and shining like gold!"

"It's OUR ship! Got to keep it neat!" John Brown added proudly.

The dawn was met by the sailing master's command "Set main topgallant!"

Peter Furnace ran along with other sailors up the main mast shrouds, the ropes supporting the mast. On his way up he slowed down and looked with horror at the narrow weather deck seventy two feet below, moving with every wave. Peter's heart began pounding, ready to jump out of the boy's chest. Noticing this, John Brown, climbing up two feet below Peter, shouted to the boy. "Peter, listen to me! Never look down. Look up! Do as I tell!"

Panting, old John moved up, followed by Peter. Finally they joined the other six seamen on the main topgallant mast head just as a new order sounded "Main topgallant – stand by!"

Peter, his eyes closed, grabbed the mast feeling dizzy. He was scared to death to let the mast go. The boy tried to open one eye, but at the sight of the deck, moving far below, shut it again. He felt the mast swaying in the fresh breeze. Peter's heart skipped a beat. It seemed his weight alone would be enough to overturn the ship.

"Main topgallant – trice up and lay out!"

Seamen spread out along the forty five feet long main topgallant yard – a spar attached to the mast with a sail bent over it, staying on a thin foot-rope beneath. Balance had to be kept with their feet on a moving foot rope and hands on the topgallant yard itself while they were laying out the heavy sail. A small mistake and Death would be inevitable.

Peter was trying to catch up with the others until the sickness came back. Overwhelmed by spasm, the powder boy began throwing up. When his hands jerked to his mouth, he lost the balance and started his fall down with a terrified scream "A-a-a-a".

By instinct, the boy endeavored to grab a rigging-rope but missed it. As lightning, thoughts of his sick mother and younger brothers, dying from hunger, passed thru his mind. "Hail Mary" slipped from his lips when a strong arm managed to grab him, placing the boy back on the topgallant yard. It was the same John Brown. The old seaman had been watching Peter from the corner of his eye, catching sight of his unusual paleness.

With his heart at his throat, the old jack tar shouted. "Always have one arm for yourself, boy! Remember, whatever ye do, have one arm for yourself!"

♣ ♣ ♣

CHAPTER 8

5th OF JULY 1812. OPEN SEA. GUN DRILL

The bell stroked 10 am. Captain Hull waited for its last sound to die before saying to Lieutenant Morris "Not too bad, the crew is getting along. Still, so much to do and no time to waste! Every man shall know exactly where he has to be during the action. Get a barrel for the gun exercise and beat to quarters!"

In no time, a drum burst out rattling. The old-timers ran straight to their stations, new-comers, however, looked lost. The boatswain's pipes and the shouts of the officers directed seamen to their assigned duty spots. The war-ship tidiness disappeared. With all four hundred fifty souls moving, the frigate looked like a disturbed ant colony.

First, everything from the spar and the gun decks had to be moved below, providing room for carronade and long gun teams. Even the privileged hens, which enjoyed the fresh air of the upper deck, had to free their spot.

"That's ok, honey-dear! Ye'll be fine in the orlop!" John Brown talked to the cackling birds trying to calm them down while carrying a coop below.

"Lord, to waste such hot coals," Old Jack, the cook, was sighing while pouring water into the galley fire to put it out as the command "beat to quarters" required.

Ivan Stone, his hands busy packing the Captain's dishes into an old sail-cloth, kept an eye on five seamen on duty to carry the Great Cabin furniture below. "Mates, ye be careful with that table! D'ye hear!"

Not ten minutes passed as all the bulkheads from the gun deck were removed. The Great Cabin disappeared, its walls dismounted and stored in the lower deck – orlop, creating a long space from bow to stern to give room for the long guns to be unfastened. Water-tubs were filled on the spar and gun decks, slow matches were started in buckets full of sand, splinter netting was set over the weather-deck.

"What's that net for?" The boy Peter Furnace asked John Brown when the two of them had finished spreading sand on the upper deck.

"I says, to save us from sharp oak splinters when the enemy's fire hits a mast or the ship's side, boy!" The old sailor explained, amused it was not obvious to a landsman. "C'mon, to our battle stations!" Brown hurried below into the gun desk, followed by the boy.

On the spar-deck a crew of five – the captain of the gun, a sponger, a fireman, a boarder and a powder-boy manned a carronade, nicknamed "the smasher" for the devastation it made at the short range. If the distance was more than a musket-shot, the carronades were useless. Long guns, however, could aim at a thousand yards, though they were very difficult to handle and required almost three times more men - fourteen sailors.

For both types the power of penetration depended on the range – the closer the more forceful, at thirty yards easily cutting 35 inch thick hard oak like it was butter, hurling a shower of sharp splinters forty yards around.

Besides shooting, a boarder in a carronade crew and two boarders in long gun team had the duty to leap on an enemy's deck armed with cutlasses, tomahawks or long pikes when the ships were alongside and the captain would shout "Boarders, away!"

A lieutenant, a midshipman, or a master's mate was in charge of each five gun-division. John Brown, a 24 pound long gun loader, respected the young lieutenant Beckman Hoffman, the commander of the starboard five guns nearest to the frigate's stern.

Lost, Peter Furnace watched seamen work to get the gun deck ready. Not sure about his duties, the boy tried to be close to the man who had saved his life, getting in everybody's way. John Brown shouted at him. "Hey, Peter, ye forgot? Ye're a powder-boy at the first gun in the starboard division! " The old seaman pointed to the gun next to his. "See that tall seaman? It's ye'r gun-captain, James Campbell! Run to the magazine and bring the powder-bag back! "

Doing his best, Peter did run below and soon returned with eight pound bag placed in a small container with a closed lid as a precaution against accidental ignition.

The boy rushed directly to his gun-captain and handed him the powder-container.

"Wait! Stay behind me!" James Campbell ordered, not taking the powder.

"Cast loose and provide!" Hull instructed thru a trumpet.

"Cast loose your gun," Beckman Hoffman echoed.

The starboard gun team unfastened the tackles at the bulwark that held their gun against the side of the ship, setting the gun free. With the carriage, it weighed nearly three tons. Should it get loose in the rough sea, a long gun could crush everything including the ship's board.

Until they fastened the side-tackles back, two men would hold them, preventing a gun from rolling.

"Level your gun!" Lieutenant Hoffman shouted.

A sponger and two boarders pushed a handspike under the gun breech and leveled it up. Gun's captain James Campbell thrust the spike under the gun, and set its barrel to the horizontal position.

After the gun's crew lifted the train tackles, James Campbell commanded "Two-six – heave! Two-six – heave," coordinating seamen's efforts hauling the gun in.

A boarder squeezed in between the gun's muzzle and the port – a hole in the ship's side, taking out the wooden tompion that plugged the muzzle, blocking sea-water.

"Load Cartridge!" Campbell cried out, making a sign to Peter Furnace "Boy, the powder-bag!"

Confused, Peter handed him a powder-bag container. "The bag! To the First Loader!" Campbell shrieked pointing to the thin seaman

With his hands shaking, the boy fished out the flannel bag from the container and handed the powder to the First loader. The loader grabbed it and, not wasting a second, inserted the bag into the muzzle. The wad – a piece of wool – immediately followed from the sponger.

Forgetting about his sea-sickness, Peter watched all the steps of gun-firing with wide-open eyes.

"Ram Cartridge!" Hoffman yelled.

Leaning out of the port, the 2nd Loader used a rammer to move the cartridge and the wad into the barrel until they reached the breech end of the gun.

"Load Round!"

In a split second, a round iron ball was snatched from a rack and shoveled into the muzzle.

"Ram Round!"

As soon as the First Loader rammed the iron ball reaching the cartridge, the powder bag was pierced by the gun captain through the touch hole with the gunner's pick –priming wire.

"Run out your gun!" Hoffman shouted.

"Two-six – heave! Two-six – heave!" The gun captain directed his crew.

The side tackles were elevated until the mizzen came out of the port-lid.

"Prime," the next order sounded from Hoffman.

Having taken the powder horn from his side, James Campbell poured a fine gun powder into the touch hole. Immediately, the sponger covered the touch hole with the flat of his hand averting accidental ignition.

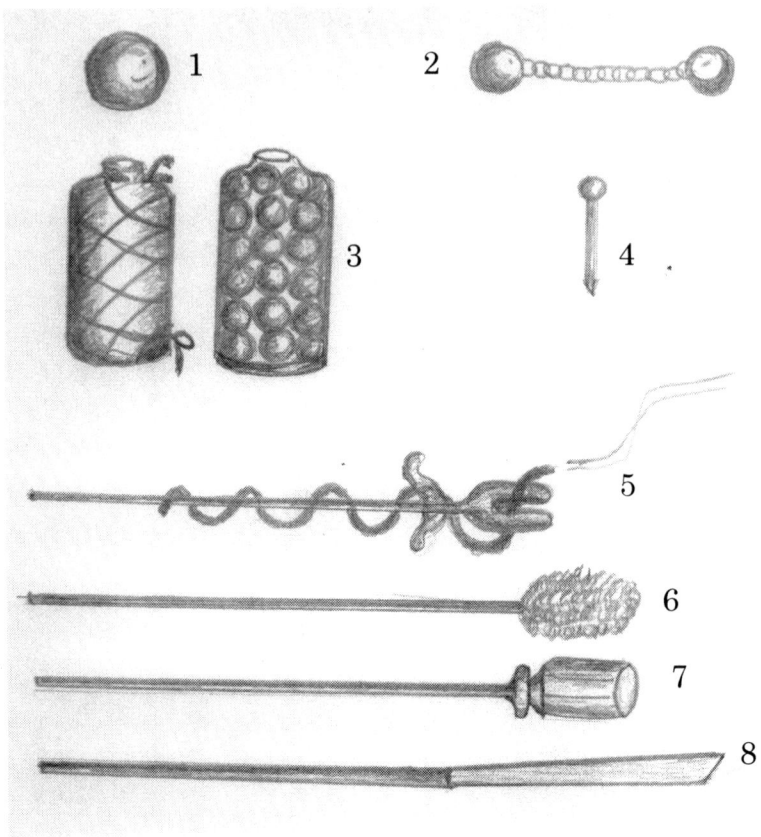

1. Round shot (24 or 32-pound metal ball).
2. Chain shot.
3. Grape shot   tightly packed metal balls into a canvas bag.
4. Gunner pick used to pierce a powder bag.
5. Linstock to hold a lighted slow match (a 3-strand cotton rope, soaked in salt peter).
6. Sponge (wool), moistened with water to mop out the interior of the barrel to eliminate sparks.

7. Rammer to move a cloth cartridge (gun powder bag), a cloth wad, a shot (e.g. a chain shot), followed by another wad.

8. Handspike to move the gun's carriage and to raise the gun's breech so the wedge-shaped quoin could be moved to adjust the gun's elevation.

"Point your gun!" Hoffman commanded.

Campbell bent over the gun and looked along its barrel. At that time, it was the only way to aim - just looking along the barrel and knowing the gun thru and thru owing to the constant drills. No sighting equipment was provided.

"Up-Up!" uttered Campbell.

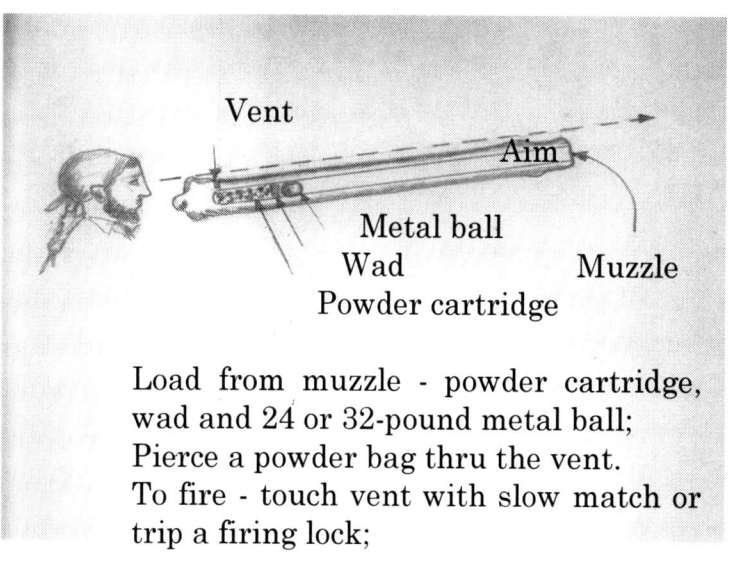

Vent

Aim

Metal ball
Wad   Muzzle
Powder cartridge

Load from muzzle - powder cartridge, wad and 24 or 32-pound metal ball;
Pierce a powder bag thru the vent.
To fire - touch vent with slow match or trip a firing lock;

Two boarders thrust their hand spikes under the breech of the gun, elevating its barrel and letting Campbell adjust the quoin – a wooden wedge. Once the correct elevation of the barrel was set, the gun captain nodded to the boarders to remove their hand spikes.

"First gun, fire!" Lt. Hoffman cried out.

"Stand by!" The gun captain yelled, making the gun crew-members move further back, while two boarders continued holding the gun side tackles, staying about eight feet distant from its barrel.

The ship guns had lanyards; however, they often failed until a gun became hot after a couple of firings. Knowing this well, James Campbell always used an old reliable slow match – a very slow burning cord. The sponger grabbed a linstock – a four-foot long staff with a fork at one end that held a lit slow match from the sand bucket, and passed it to the gun captain.

Staying three feet from the gun, Campbell brought the burning slow-match to the touch hole, then instantly turned his head away.

A hissing sound, a flash and the gun fired with a deafening boom, jumping four feet backwards between the two men who continued to hold the side tackles.

Terrified, Peter Furnace grasped his ears and dropped to his knees – he had never heard such a thundering roar before.

At once thick gray smoke covered everything, bringing tears and coughs to the crew men and dirtying their faces with black powder dust.

Wiping his eyes with the back of his hands, Campbell rushed to peer thru the port – he needed to see the ball's trajectory to correct the gun's elevation.

One after another the other four guns of the Lieutenant Hoffman's division fired, as directed by his command.

Captain Hull, staying on the quarter-deck, watched the balls flying, followed by white smoke streaming to the leeward. All of them dropped into the sea far from the target barrel. The other gun divisions' results were no less disappointing.

"No good! Repeat!" The Captain ordered – the crew had to be trained before the frigate would join the squadron. And Hull was running out of time.

♣ ♣ ♣

CHAPTER 9

5th OF JULY 1812. OPEN SEA.
SQUEAKING JOHN

On the first day at sea the officers invited their Captain to supper while they still had fresh provisions available.

Wooden plates with green onions, cucumbers, corn bread, a big plate with fried fish, another one with ham and smoked beef tongue brought a colorful touch to the war-ship's scenery.

Officers did not possess wine glasses, so tin mugs were used. Staying behind the Captain's chair, Ivan Stone poured wine into his master's mug first.

Hull nodded to the old servant then gazed at the table "Thank you, officers, this is a feast! Wish we always had fresh food! On a long cruise we have to satisfy ourselves eating salted meat every day and dreaming about plum duff. Ha-ha. What landsman would be keen on flour boiled with water?"

Finishing laughing, Hull raised his mug high "For the Constitution!"

"Yes indeed! For the Constitution!" joined the officers.

"Sir, you promised to tell us about Squeaking John and why he brings luck?" Morris asked, addressing the Captain.

All the others looked puzzled - they had not heard anything of this matter yet.

"Pass the word to Squeaking John!" Hull told his servant.

Stone caught Squeaking John in the seamen berth next to the wardroom and they came back together without any delay. Approaching the table, Squeaking John snatched his hat and saluted the officers.

"John, tell us the story how you became 'Squeaking John' and why you bring luck." Hull asked. Then he turned to his servant, "Ivan, a chair for Squeaking John!"

The old seaman looked at the officers, and then took a seat, clearing his throat before starting his tale.

"Sirs, on my seventeenth birthday, I joined Joseph Hull, our Captain's father, the brave man! Right after the 'Jersey'-prison, sick as hell, he found a couple of small boats. 'Cause we could not bite the British, but we could mighty annoy them! Ha-ha! Once a fisherman told us that a wood supply boat was loaded at Bronx ready for Manhattan. Hull decided to capture it at night. Upon my soul, it was not that difficult 'cause the British ain't expect us there, they, bloody bastards, begging ye'r pardon, sirs, felt quite at home on our shores! We left our schooner at sea, and sailed small boats to the bay as we were fishermen."

No officers but Hull had heard about that day before. Complete silence fell at the table as the old sailor continued his story.

"It was dark that night. We had 'bout twenty men in three small fishing boats. Avoiding any noise, we sailed into the bay and got alongside a large supply boat. Then we climbed up onto its deck.

Nicholas Orloff

A British sentinel, drunken as a pig, moonshine no doubt, fell down, his throat cut. Then the turn of another British came. Quickly we heaved the boat's anchor and started out of the bay where an enemy's armed schooner was moored."

John paused then continued, "Oh, ye, I was scared all right. They could sink us in a wink, armed with a carronade. But pray the Lord - the British sentinel didn't raise the alarm as he recognized their ship. When our supply boat's getting closer and the ships could collide, the British watcher shouted 'Ship, ahoy! Have a care!' "

'Don't worry, room enough!' Captain Joseph Hull cried out. Ye know, sirs, what a brave man, his voice did not even tremble! Our Captain, God bress his soul, kept sailing close to the schooner bow. When our boat touched it, Hull whispered 'Go away!' He wanted to take it by surprise. We crossed ourselves and leapt onto the British schooner armed with boarding axes, cutlasses, and muskets. As I jumped on the British board, the watcher slashed my belly with a cutlass."

John stopped. A fly buzzed, circling above the ham leftovers. It was the only sound in the wardroom besides the ship noise – the officers were all ears.

"I ain't remember how I dropped down on the deck. But I remember the pain. I tried to hold in my bowels, laying there in the pool of blood. My fingers were getting numb and could hardly hold my guts. Blood was pulsing from my throat too. I knew my last minutes on Earth were near..."

Squeaking John drew a long sigh. "After that I ain't remember nothing, and will tell what my friend Caleb Smith told me later. Captain Joseph Hull shot the watcher on the spot. Woken by the noise, the British captain in his night shirt jumped on his schooner's deck just to get a musket ball in his heart. We seized the rest of the British sailors, heaved their small boats aboard the schooner, unmoored it and with the supply boat sailing alongside headed out of the bay to Black Rock, that's Connecticut."

The story-teller looked at the officers around the table and continued his story.

"We had to sneak past three British ships on Long Island. Our luck, they recognized their own ships and ain't suspect anything. Upon my soul, dear Sirs, I ain't see that - I ain't was in my senses. My dear chap, Caleb Smith, God bress his soul, was grasping my belly, keeping my bowels in... He had to use all his strength 'cause my guts were pushing out so hard..."

Squeaking John stopped for a while as if still feeling the same pain as during those horrible hours. He involuntary grasped his belly but then, feeling no pain, relaxed and smiled.

"God, can't forget that! When we got into Connecticut, Angels watched over me. A captured English surgeon saved my life. Ye know, Sirs, he used spirit of wine on my belly while sewing me up and Caleb told me that then he rubbed spirit of wine on my wound every day! Although I could not see nor feel it 'cause I ain't was myself. Otherwise I'd rather drink it!"

Everybody at the table laughed heartily. Ivan Stone, staying behind the Captain's chair, giggled too, displaying many missing teeth the old sailor lost when scurvy flourished on a whaling cruise. It was a common thing: after two-three years in the Pacific around Cape Horn without any greens, the whaler-ships came home with a jug containing hundreds of the crew's teeth.

Meanwhile the teller continued. "I got better and my throat healed too but started squeaking, so now people call me Squeaking John. But I ain't mind it!"

Still laughing, Hull poured some wine for Squeaking John "A toast to you, John, and your strong bowels!" Then he said to others "This guy's got guts!"

Everybody smiled.

"Spirit of wine on an abdominal wound? I wonder why? And why not? Might be useful one day!" The ship's surgeon Evans said with amazement on his face.

"It's a miracle you survived such wounds!" Morris wondered shaking his head.

"That's why, Sirs, they say I bring luck!" Squeaking John declared.

"Maybe, you will bring luck to the Constitution then!" First Lieutenant Morris proclaimed.

"Hear, hear!" All cried out, raising their mugs.

♣ ♣ ♣

CHAPTER 10

8th OF JULY 1812. OPEN SEA.
A PIECE OF SALTED MEAT

A new target barrel, set in the sea, started another gun training session.

A drum rattling called seamen to their stations. After three days of drills, they already knew what should they do and where should they be.

"Run out your gun! Fire!" Hull commanded, lifting his hand.

One of the balls missed the target by several yards only, raising sailors' cheers.

At dusk the sounds of "The Liverpool girls" song were heard on the forecastle. One man started:

"When I was a youngster I sailed with th' rest
On a Liverpool packet bound out to th' west.
We anchored a day in the harbour o' Cork,
Then put out to sea for th' port o' New York."

His mates joined in chorus:

An' it's Ho! Ro! Ho, bullies, ho!
Th' Liverpool Gir-ils have got us in tow."

Seaman John Brown came to the deck, looked around as if searching for somebody, and headed to the boy Peter Furnace, who sat on the deck floor motionless with lifeless face, no strength left to sing with others. Smiling, John Brown handed him out a piece of un-cooked salted meat – an old seamen's remedy for sea-sickness.

"Sickness's gone? Here, Peter, have some meat! Eat it all! It'll bring your strength back!"

"Thankee ye kindly, sir!" sniffled Peter.

Being hungry with his stomach washed out with throwing up, the boy greedily took the meat and started gnawing at it, forgetting about anything else.

Other seamen smiled even though they knew their dinner tomorrow would lack this pound of beef - the purser strictly followed the Admiralty's instruction to provide four pounds of salted beef and two pounds of pork with bones and skin a week for each seaman. Not an ounce more. Besides stale ship biscuits, a pound of dry pies and a pound of beans a week, salted meat was the crew's main food. Old Jack – the cook would soak the meat in the evening to get rid of its salt for tomorrow's dinner.

On a crowded ship no secrets could be kept, and today everybody knew John Brown asked Old Jack about this piece of meat for the boy, following the seamen brothership rule to share if their mate needed it badly.

"Don't ye worry, kid, we all were sea-sick the first day at sea!" Daniol Lewis winked to Peter.

"Not many fell from the tops though," cook Old Jack added. "Ye are lucky to be alive, boy!"

♣ ♣ ♣

CHAPTER 11

16th OF JULY 1812. OPEN SEA.
A CASE OF MADEIRA

That evening the officers, invited by the Captain for supper, sat at the Great Cabin's table covered with a white table cloth - all the frigate's lieutenants, Master John Alwyn, and Surgeon Amos A. Evans. Midshipman German was also invited. The officers were silent, working hard on ham and cheese from the Captain's private pantry.

Hull worked hard too, never missing a chance to eat to his heart's content. Finally he swallowed the last piece of cheese on his plate, and said "...Ten days at sea. Tomorrow we'll join the squadron. I hope, the Admiralty orders us to fight!"

"Excuse me sir, do you think we are up to the task to fight the British? They've had the sea for twenty years, beating the French, Spaniards, and Dutch?" Morris asked.

"Yes, we can. US frigates are fast and big ships in their class. We carry 24-pounders, the British frigates have just 18. We are a good match, one on one."

"Sir, do you think the Constitution can outsail a British frigate? I read an article in the 'Times', they laughed at our ships." Second Lieutenant Alexander Wardsworth asked.

"They laugh because they are ignorant. Let me tell you something... One year after the Constitution was launched Captain Parker of HMS Santa Margareta on his way from Madeira paid us a visit. He thought the Constitution's design was so unusual that he suggested a bet that Santa Margareta would easily outsail us. Our Captain accepted the challenge and next morning both ships started the race. In one hour Santa Margareta fell behind and Captain Parker was obliged to send a boat with a case of fine Madeira! Ha-ha. The best I ever tasted!"

The company at the table burst with laughter.

"Beg your pardon, sir, but the Constitution is getting old, she is fifteen now, isn't she?" Midshipman German asked.

"She is but perfect as can be. Her hull was thoroughly scraped, and new copper-patches were put on." Hull looked at his officers and said firmly "We meet the enemy frigate, take the challenge and win! To the Constitution!"

"To the Constitution!" Everybody at the table shouted, raising their glasses.

♣ ♣ ♣

CHAPTER 12

17th OF JULY 1812. OPEN SEA.
THEY ARE ALL BRITISH, ALL FIVE OF THEM

The ship's bell struck four -2 pm when the mast head watch cry "Quarterdeck, ahoy, ship ho!" interrupted the clothes washing going on the deck done once a week. Seamen, wooden clothes pegs in their mouths, stopped hanging laundry on the line and turned.

"Where away?" shouted Hull from the quarter-deck.

"Four sails to the Northward! In shore of us!" mast head watch replied from 90 feet above.

"What kind of ships?" the Captain hollered out.

"Can't make it out! Too far!"

Captain Hull quickly took off his hat and coat, jumped into the shrouds and ran up the ratlines more like a boy than a forty year old man. Having reached the masthead, he sat there, both arms hooked around the topgallant rigging. From this spot over ten miles in each direction could be seen with four small white clouds of sails against the dark hazy shore of New Jersey (Egg Harbor, near Atlantic City) to the North. Too far away to make out what ships they were.

Having checked the other sides of the horizon with nothing there but the endless blue and calm sea, the Captain ran down to the quarterdeck. "Too big for merchants and heading westward to the shore. Men-of-war, no doubt. My guess it is our squadron! No way could the British make it from Halifax in ten days," Hull told Lt. Morris, "Let's meet the squadron. Course North-North-East!"

The First Lieutenant touched his hat in salute and passed the command to the helmsman "Set course North-North-East!"

"All hands, about ship," cried out the Captain.

In a wink, seamen rushed up from the hatches to make sails. Their Captain could be proud watching them work. The crew knew their business perfectly having been drilled several times every a day to set, reef and take in sails.

The bell tolled eight: 4 pm, calling the First dog watch up, when another mast-watch cry split the calm "On deck there, ship ho! A ship hull-down bearing North East under all sails. Looks like man-of-war."

Through his telescope, best on the ship, the Captain could see a small white spot glowing on the North horizon.

"Too far. Those four in shore ships could be seen just from the mast head. Can it be the frigate Belvidere, supposed to be in these waters? We might try to catch her! Lt. Morris, let the crew have their dinner! No good to start the battle with empty bellies!"

At sundown the Constitution, all sails set, was heading North East with the fifth ship still too far to make out if it was a Yankee or a British ship.

"In-shore four ships are Southward and Eastward. Let's stand for the fifth ship. It is getting closer: about eight miles distance," Hull pointed to his First

Lieutenant. Then he commanded "Mr. Alwyn, haul down the staysails. Set the spanker!"

Once executed, another order came "Let's beat to quarters!"

Lieutenant Morris piped out "Beat to quarters! Clear the ship for action!"

At the sound of the drum, all sailors jumped from the hatches, clearing the decks and taking their positions.

Complete dark fell around 10 pm with all seamen either on the spar or the gun deck, ready for action. All ears, they were waiting for a word from the Captain.

"Lieutenant Read, private signal to the unknown ship!" shouted Hull.

Three directional light lanterns in the form of a triangle were set on the foremast at once, and Lieutenant Read began sending the frigate's private number with a blue directional light lantern.

Isaac Hull attentively watched the ship that sent no signal in reply. "Could it be they didn't receive our signal, the distance still being too big? " Captain's mind was racing, "Keep sending signals!"

An hour later Hull and Morris, as the rest of the crew, still were on the upper-deck watching the dim lights of the approaching ship when Lieutenant Read saluted "Sir, it won't signal back."

"Could not answer the signal?" Captain Hull bit his lip in the thoughtful revelation... Confirming his worst dread, the unknown ship made a signal: one blue racket and two gun-shots – not US Navy signal. "Damn, they're all British, all five of them! Look, that ship is making signals to the others a shore!

Our intelligence was wrong – the enemy squadron was not in Halifax!"

"We are in BIG trouble!" murmured Hull to himself, then loud "Set the course South-South-East. Make all sails!"

"All hands about ship!" repeated the command Mr. Alwyn, boatswain Adams pipe calls followed.

Through his night spy-glass the Captain saw the unknown ship changing her course in chase of the Constitution and signaling to the in shore ships. "Good, they left their lights on – they're too confident. Well," he posed "...this is the Yankee they won't catch."

"Silence fore and aft! Douse all lights! Change the course 20 points South!" commanded the Yankee Captain.

Before he finished his order, the lights went off, surrendering the Constitution to complete darkness. The officers and the crew watched the unknown ship looking for their location.

"Sir, do you think we might get away clear?" Morris asked in a troubled voice.

"Not likely, the breeze is not strong enough for us to make a good distance. Five ships spread out make a wide net to catch us. In the morning we'll see how lucky we are!"

♣ ♣ ♣

CHAPTER 13

18th OF JULY 1812. OPEN SEA. KEDGING

In the dusk before sunrise Hull, heavy bags under his eyes, was standing on the quarterdeck. He and the crew were up all night working hard reefing, trying to outsail the enemy ships, uncertain of their exact location in the hazy night air. "Ship ho!" shouted the mast-head watch, tearing apart the stillness of the upcoming morning.

"Where away?"

"Two frigates under our lee! More sails astern five or six miles distant!" The troubled voice dropped from the above.

Ten minutes had not passed before the dim light of the approaching sunrise unveiled two frigates downwind from the Yankee frigate, at seven or eight miles.

The beginning of that heavenly summer day with almost no wind did not cheer up the Yankee souls. The Constitution sails were empty, hanging like rugs. The Captain and his First Lieutenant ran up to the mast head. Having trained their spy-glasses, they watched a frigate five miles astern followed by a ship of the line- a two decker, another frigate, and two smaller ones.

"All enemy ships! We could fight one-on-one, but five ships..." Hull turned to Morris his troubled face. "...No other choice, we have to flee!"

Half an hour later the morning haziness had almost gone, lifting the horizon.

"Those two under our lee are the frigates Belvidere and Aeolus. The first one astern is the frigate Guerriere. Obviously chasing us and moving fast. Look, they still have a nice breeze!" Hull smacked his fist into his open hand. "It's so darn calm here!"

At 6 am eight bells sounded, sending a second dog watch up in the rigging. The night watch stayed on the forecastle, waiting for orders.

"Let starboard watch have their breakfast, something fast. Mr. Purser, I believe that double ration of cheese could be provided!" told Hull to Chew.

Boatswain piped breakfast. Sailors went down and soon were back with ship biscuits, and a small piece of goat cheese. Breaking the biscuits into tiny pieces, the seamen chewed slowly, all eyes on the enemy ships. The larboard watch was relieved by the starboard shift to get some breakfast too. The last wind died. The Constitution, her head toward the enemy ships, stopped motionless, two British under her lee.

In the complete silence seaman James Frances muttered to himself.

"Down dropped the breeze,
The sails dropped down
'Twas sad as sad could be;
And we did speak only to break
The silence of the sea!"

Captain Hull's mind was racing over how to save the ship "Mr. Morris, the wind failed us! Let's use

Yankee muscles since the Gods have left! Have the boats hoisted out at once!"

Sailors ran to the boats and unhooked the tackles. Adams' orders followed "Lay aloft! Lay out! Trice up! Man the stays! Lower away all, d'ye hear?"

A long-boat, two cutters and two whale-boats were lowered. "Tie the end of the cable to beams at the head. Coxswains, tie the other cable's end to your boats!" ordered Alwyn.

"I hate rowing," said Asa Curtis, a seaman in the long boat, spitting on his hands.

"Ye better like it. It's gonna save our arse today," grinned John Brown, sitting next to Curtis.

Taking the tiller at the stern of the long boat, the coxswain coordinated the oarsmen "Stand By Oars! Toss Oars! Let Fall! Prepare to Give Way!"

Men leaned forward and extended their arms, holding the oar clear of the water and ready to row.

"Give Way Together! Oars! Pick up the Stroke," commanded the coxswain.

Leaning back and skillfully using the body more than the arms, oarsmen dipped their blades and began pulling. They followed the rhythm set by the coxswain, lifting the oars clear of the water when recovering.

The long boat started moving slowly. Towing such a big ship as the Constitution demanded enormous effort. The oars were creaking with applied force and men were groaning, straining their muscles, forgetting about their limits. Under the bright July sun, humid and still air didn't cool off the skin. Soaking wet handkerchiefs covered the seamen heads, letting sweat stream down their faces. Both hands busy rowing, all they could do was to close their eyes for a quick second and jerk their heads sharply, forcing the sweat in all directions.

When the burned-out seamen began slowing down, one of them murmured "It's the end... I ain't rowing more," the black sailor James Frances shouted, tearing apart his dried out throat "Mates, remember 'Jersey'-prison? Pull! Pull, the bastards will not catch us ever!"

His white friend Daniel Lewis added "Better die rowing than be in a British prison again!"

"Aye, mates, aye," answered hoarse voices.

As though given a fresh push, sailors pulled on their oars overcoming exhaustion. Slowly but steadily, the boat turned left, forcing the Constitution head to gradually move in the same direction, away from the Belvidere and the Aeolus.

Having finished sail trimming, seamen Hogan and Cheever stepped down on the main mast top.

"Lookee here, mate, we are turnin' away! We still have a chance!" Hogan said.

"Yea!" a tiny smile lighted up Cheever's face, "But wait... lookee, de bastards are lowerin' deir boats too!"

Horror-stricken, seamen watched all British boats heading to the frigates Shannon and Belvidere, the ships nearest to the Constitution.

Soon ten boats started towing the Shannon! The Belvidere was towed by nine! The distance between the enemy and the Constitution began decreasing fast with the Shannon only four-five miles away.

"De dam villains are gainin' on us!" Hogan said in alarm to Cheever.

"Dear Jesus and Mother of God, help us! Ain't dere any hope?"

Hull, his face as gloomy as a dark cloud, was watching the enemy ships through the old spy-glass.

"Ship-of-the-line Africa, the old 64-gun ship under Captain John Bastard. The leading frigate is the Shannon, British squadron flag-ship, Captain Broke, one of the best captains in the British Navy, no doubt about that. The others are frigates Aeolis, Guerriere and Belvidere." Hull said to Morris, then pointing at the brig, "that brig and the schooner are definitely ours, probably taken as prizes! And here we are! Four frigates along with a two-decker and no wind! We are in a nice pickle!"

"Right, Sir! No hope left. Should we strike?" asked Morris, shooting a desperate glance at the enemy's ships.

Sailors, looking anxiously at their Captain, tried to catch every word from the officers on the quarterdeck. They had surely heard Lt. Morris's suggestion to surrender.

"Fight for our freedom, son" - his dying father's last words – passed thru Hull's mind. "This Yankee would not surrender!" Hull said loud and then even louder - for sailors to hear - "Lieutenant Morris, there is always hope at sea, especially with such a great ship as the Constitution!"

Fast as seagulls, the Captain's words flew around the ship being spread from one sailor to another. On the forecastle Old Jack, the cook, turned to the other seamen "Captain says there's still hope!"

A hundred feet above the deck seaman Hogan, almost smiling with tears sparkling in his eyes, mouthed "Captain says dere's still hope!"

Meanwhile the enemy was getting closer, dangerously closer, a little more and the Shannon could fire her eighteen-ponders right into the most vulnerable part of the Constitution – her stern, raking the Yankee from stern to bows.

"Lt. Morris, get one long gun from gun-deck and run it out aft as a stern chaser. Cut the stern frame and run out two twenty-fours from the gun-deck at the Great Cabin windows!"

At once, the boatswain's pipes sounded their call, sending sailors into the dismounted Great Cabin.

"Clear for Action," followed. Ten days of constant training had paid off - all sailors took their stations on the upper or gun decks in no time.

"Silence fore and aft!" Alwyn hollered.

With no wind in the sails, a deathly hush dropped over the frigate. Even on the gun deck, sailors could clearly hear their Captain's words.

"Shipmates! The British have invaded our country again. Want to lose our freedom and be slaves for the kingdom?"

"No! No way!" All crew shouted back as one.

"Let's fight for our Constitution!"

The roar "For our Constitution! Huzzah!" filled up the decks and rigging. Tears, hope and the wish to save the frigate brightened the faces of the crew.

"Lieutenant Hoffman, Shannon is close to gun-range. Try one stern gun. See if we can reach her!" Hull told Lieutenant Hoffman.

Hoffman rushed into the Great Cabin "Cast loose your gun- Level you gun - out tompion!"

"Two-six – heave! Two-six – heave!" Gun's Captain James Campbell shrieked.

The crew ran the long gun in for about a foot. The carved and painted tompion that plugged the gun muzzle was taken out.

"Load Cartridge – Ram Cartridge – Load Round – Ram - Run out your gun!" Hoffman was crying out.

"Two-six – heave! Two-six – heave!" Campbell shouted.

The muzzle went out of the port-lid when a new command from the Lieutenant followed, "Prime-Point your gun. Aim at the towing boats!"

"Begging you pardon, Sir? Did you say "Aim at the boats"? Ain't it not civilized?" The gun's captain James Campbell asked, amazement on his face.

"Like I care – THEY are chasing us, not I! Fire!" barked Hoffman.

A hissing sound, a flash and thundering roar of a firing gun, and nothing could be seen thru the powder smoke that filled the gun deck. Above, on the spar deck, Hull watched the ball drop into the sea with a big splash 300 yards before the Shannon's first towing boat. Panicking, sailors in the boat stopped rowing, then in haste turned the boat head to the coming wave, born by the ball. When the wave lifted their boat and was gone, the British went back to rowing, much less eager in the chase.

"No more firing. We can not reach them. The lead if you please." Hull shouted; a worried look plastered on his face.

At the same moment the Shannon opened fire from her bow guns, none of her balls reaching the Constitution yet. Fortunately, all Yankee towing boats were protected from the enemy fire by the Constitution itself. Soon the Shannon stopped shooting her guns.

"Sir, twenty four fathoms, sand and shell." Midshipmen German reported up to Lt. Morris.

The First Lieutenant rushed to the Captain. "Sir, just twenty four fathoms! We can kedge!"

That brought a light smile on Hull's face "Good thinking, Charles! Signal the blue cutter to come back to get a kedging anchor. Get the long cable prepared!"

Sailors knotted pieces of thick ropes and cables together. Young Peter Furnace tried being useful keeping close to his rescuer. "John Brown, what's kedging?"

"A kedge's a small anchor 'bout 400 pounds. We use it to get out of harbor against the tide or the current. We drop the anchor into water 'bout 200 yards in the needed direction, and use many hands here on the deck to drag the ship forward. Much faster than the towing boats can do!"

The blue cutter was back in no time. Once the dog-tired crew had climbed up into the Constitution, the sailors collapsed on the deck. Their shipmates brought them tin mugs full of water.

A fresh shift headed the cutter to where the kedging anchor had already been placed. The other boats were still struggling with their towing.

"Do your best, mates! Our Constitution is in YOUR hands," cried out Alwyn to the sailors in the cutter.

The blue boat was gliding ahead of the Yankee frigate. "Oar. Pull. Pull for our Constitution!" coxswain sent the orders and the sailors did pull, tearing their muscles above human limits. They were soaking wet and roasting under the blazing burning sun. Their heavy breath, their gasps for air covered the sound of the splashes under the oars.

"Rig the capstan! Bring to the messenger! Man the bars!" shouted Hull on the Constitution spar-deck.

Some sailors attached the cable to the capstan; the others inserted wooden bars, and took their places, with three men on each of the eight capstan's bars.

The powder-boy Peter Furnace tried his best, working side by side with Seaman Brown, not daring to ask a question. John Brown, having noticed a puzzled look in the boy's eyes, said "Ye know what capstan's for? We will pull the cable and it will save our muscles!" The boy nodded and started dragging even harder.

At last the blue cutter with the kedging anchor was five hundred yards ahead of the frigate with no more rope left. The coxswain and two more sailors struggled dropping the four hundred pound anchor overboard while Hull watched from the forecastle. As soon as the anchor sank deep, a new order followed "Mr. Morris, start pulling!

The First Lieutenant turned to the capstan "Ready for heaving around! Heave around! Do better than that! Heave and pawl! Get all you can!"

The sailors, muscles strained tight, pushed the bars furiously, grunting, without the usual capstan shanty. The Constitution began moving, cheered by the seamen on the forecastle. Still, Morris insisted "Heave and pawl! Get all you can!"

Sailing master Alwyn replaced Lt. Morris at the capstan "Pull, pull for your life, mates!"

The efforts were not in vain: the distance between Constitution and her chasers began increasing notably. No time to catch a breath though, "Get another kedging anchor into green cutter!" Hull commanded Morris.

When the Constitution was about a hundred yards from the first kedge, the second boat started moving with another kedging anchor on its stern.

Being relieved from the hard labor, dead-thirsty old James Frances went to look for water but discovered the bucket empty. Having lifted it with his tired and shaking hands, he only got the last two drops into his mouth. Not knowing that Alwyn was behind his back, James Frances recited a piece of a poem.

> "The silly buckets on the
> deck,
> That had so long
> remained,
> I dreamt that they were
> filled with dew;
> And when I awoke, it
> rained."

"The Rime Of The Ancient Mariner", I suppose?" Alwyn asked, surprised to hear poetry from a common seaman! "How do you know it?"

"Aye, sir! Our Captain's father taught me the whole poem in Brooklyn prison 'Jersey' when I was a kid," the seaman answered, smiling politely.

As soon as the second anchor went deep, fresh men took their positions at the capstan's bars. Their worn-out mates dropt on the deck nearby, among them the old thin Captain's steward. Sailors gulped the water brought by powder-boys, and their spirits got a fresh boost.

Ivan Stone wiped sweat from his forehead "Gosh, so tired!"

Recalling something and wishing to humor his mates who were lying motionless next to him, the steward began telling an anecdote.

"Hey, lads, want my story? An old crook goes along the road, takes a seat and says "Gosh, I got so old and so tired, like a miserable piece of shit! After a while he takes his way and after a couple of yards being too tired to walk, he sits down again and repeats "Gosh, I got so old and so tired, like a miserable piece of shit! ...When young I was," – the crook stops, thinks, and says-"...still a miserable piece of shit I was!"

Exhausted sailors stretched on the deck nearby cracked with laughter, sniffing and wiping their eyes with the back of their hands. The small joke returned strength to their fatigued bodies. Moses Smith laughed until tears started sparkling on his skinny cheeks "Ha-ha-ha! Our turn to pull! Just thirty minutes - we can do it, mates!" He scrambled to his feet. "Those bastards will not catch us!"

Nicholas Orloff

♣ ♣ ♣

CHAPTER 14

18th OF JULY 1812. OPEN SEA.
YANKEES DON'T HAVE A CHANCE!

Captain Byron of British frigate "Belvidere" was watching the USS frigate, trying to understand why it suddenly gained in speed having four boats against ten British. Then he caught the sun's reflection on the Constitution's kedging anchor when it was pushed overboard.

"Oh, my, they are kedging!" exclaimed Byron, "wow, Yankees know seamanship?"

"Get the kedging anchors ready!" shouted the Captain to his officers. "Signal to the flag-ship – the Constitution is using kedging anchors!"

The Yankees were also keeping an eye on the British and noticed their new maneuver "Look, British are imitating us – they are getting their kedging anchors prepared! Smart bastards, they got all the boats to warp just two ships!" A half an hour later Hull was saying to Morris in a low troubled voice.

"See, the Belvidere is working two kedge anchors at the same time! She is gaining on us! Of course, Byron got men from the other frigates aboard! And Belvidere is a lighter ship!" Hull pointed to the nearest enemy vessel.

"How to save the ship? What else could I do? And where the hell is our squadron? British sail near New York as if it were their sea" These thoughts raced thru the Captain's mind.

"We don't have another choice but pumping water out of the main hold to lighten the ship!" Hull commanded Morris, taking a deep breath.

Following the boatswain's pipes, sailors pumped furiously, trying not to think what they were going to drink before reaching land, as the fresh water jetted overboard.

Seaman John Brown leaned over and, making a dipper with his hands, caught some water pouring overboard and drank it like it was for the last time in his life.

"John Brown, there's still water in the bucket!" Peter Furnace pointed at the deck.

"Ye, lad, ain't know what it means to be without water at sea, I can't help it!"

The distance between the brave frigate and the Shannon continued notably decreasing. Now all British boats were towing just one ship - the Shannon!

"Was there any hope left? Or were our efforts spent in vain?" All the crew was thinking.

Unlike the Yankees, the English sailors in Shannon towing boats didn't work themselves to death.

"They pressed me from a Nantucket whaler, why would I care to tow?" cried out one sailor, John Dickinson, but what he really wanted to say was "Stop rowing". He knew even what he said would kill his English mates' enthusiasm.

"Keep your trap shut up, you Nantucket pig!" barked the boat's coxswain, trembling with rage, his face purple. "Pull, mates, pull! This Yankee frigate will make a nice prize. I guess two months pay!"

"Yankees have no chance anyway! Why shall we kill ourselves towing hard?" A British seaman with a red handkerchief around his neck asked.

"Four frigates and a two-decker against a single scared Yankee? In an hour all will be over! Ha-ha!" Another one grinned.

Eager to finish the chase, the Belvidere started her broadside, the balls dropping between the Constitution and British towing boats, cooling their desire to reach the American frigate. Being torn in pieces by their own fire did not appeal to the chasers. Still, they outnumbered the Yankee boats and their Shannon was coming close... Dangerously close... Soon she would pass within gun range...

Suddenly a light breeze sprang up, filling the Constitution sails. Hull, knowing the frigate better than anyone else, took the helm, getting the best out of that opportunity.

"Why is the Captain at the helm?" midshipman Greenlaw asked midshipman German, surprise on his face – the helm was not a captain's duty.

"He knows what he does! He has known the frigate for fifteen years! More than that, Hull refitted the ship after admiral Rogers rejected the Constitution as a piece of junk".

"The Captain also set sky poles, letting her carry more and higher canvas. He had the "split" dolphin striker put in, no other ship has it!" Lt. Morris joined.

"Didn't you know Hull reduced the ship's ballast by a third and moved all the masts into the best locations?

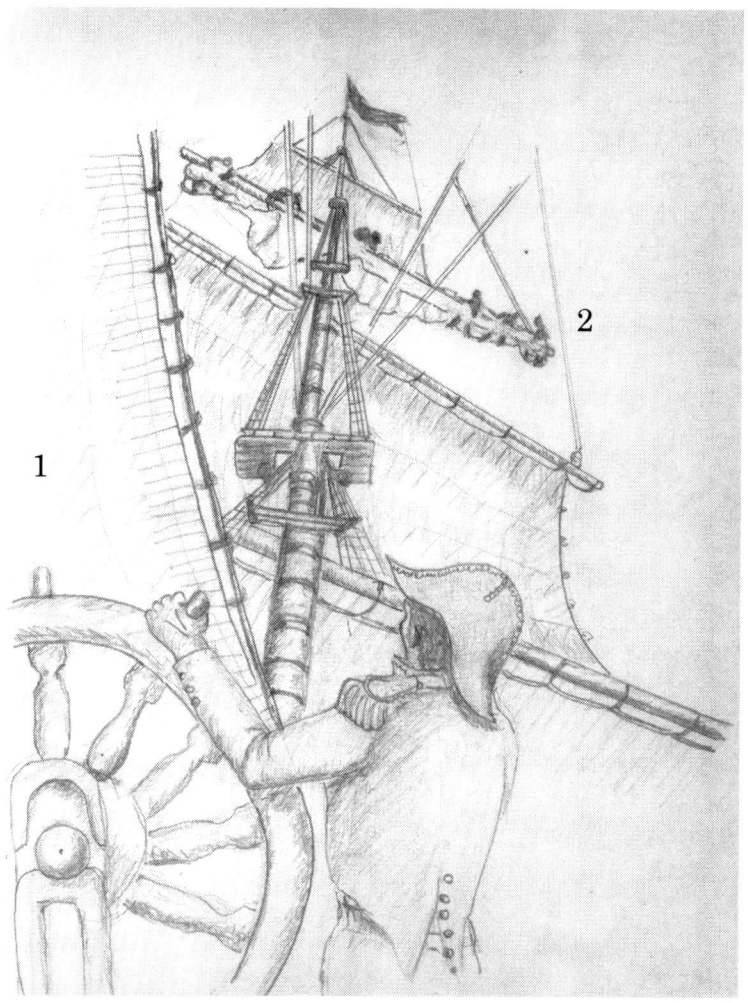

1. Maintop – a 21-foot by 16-foot platform used by the crew to fire down at the deck of enemy ships.
2. Seamen set the topgallant sail (90 feet above the deck). To set the royal or the sky sails, they had to climb even higher.

Therefore the Constitution sails faster than ever before!" Alwyn could not help but add.

With a slight wind slowly pushing the Yankee ship and her boats continue to tow, the Constitution was still ahead of her chasers, with three enemy frigates very close astern. Suddenly Belvidere caught a slight wind and glided closer.

"Damn, why has the Belvidere caught the wind?" cried Seaman Daniel Lewis to Ivan Stone.

The old servant was fast to reply "I'll give thee a wind!" He clapped his rear and farted.

Sailors, who heard that little conversation, burst out laughing. The Old Jack, the cook, laughed so hard, he doubled over. Where did they get the strength after all that murderous labor?

Still chuckling, seamen headed to relieve their mates in the returning tow boat. Twenty hours without resting, still the tide of their enthusiasm to save the ship, their dear Constitution, had not died.

In no time fresh sailors went into the cutter, among them Old Jack the cook, and even the Purser, Mr. Chew.

Seaman Reynolds, who shared the boat's bench with the Purser, looked at him with surprise – no officers row boats! Ever! With respect Reynolds handled Mr. Chew a piece of an old rug. "Mr. Purser! Bind this over ye'r hands! An important detail when ye'r hands are not used to rowing!"

"Attention to details is very important!" The Purser said in a lecturing voice without a smile.

On the gun the deck the powder boy Peter Furnace brought ship biscuits and a piece of cheese to his favorite sailor John Brown, collapsed between the long guns. "Here, John Brown, have a bite!"

"Can't eat, bone-dry. Fetch I some water, shipmate!" The old sailor whispered with parched mouth, hardly to be heard.

Proud to be called "shipmate", Peter quickly got water and handed a tin mug to the seaman. The sailor's hands shook, spilling water on his chest while he was drinking. "Thankee ye kindly, Peter, much better now!" The old sailor mouthed and started throwing up as the result of overwork and dehydration.

"What a day! Will it come to an end? Can't wait till night," everybody on Yankee ship was thinking.

Finally the blue cutter came alongside the Constitution's starboard. Trembling shadows of sailors climbed up. The purser Mr. Chew left his oar and looked at his aching hand: all the skin had gone from his palm...

At that moment enemy sailors were climbing up the Shannon, having finished their towing. One, pressed from Nantucket whaler, John Dickinson, tried a trick to help the Yankee ship. Climbing the stairs and, as if having slipped, he fell into the sea and dived with the risk of being crushed between the frigate's side and the towing boat. Being good at diving and swimming since he was a boy, Dickenson never let the English know that, hoping to have a chance to escape one day. A thunderous shout "Man overboard" ordered the towing boat to fetch the sailor out of the water, delaying the Shannon for about thirty minutes! Half an hour – it was a huge relief for the Constitution's desperate situation!

At 11 pm in the complete darkness Hull still had the helm, constantly watching the small wind and giving orders to reef sails accordingly. Even the night could not stop the Yankees: seamen kept towing the boats. Those who were not rowing or setting sails stayed on the spar or gun decks. Many fell fast asleep wherever they found a spot.

The first watch was up in the rigging, ready to make sails when a fresh breeze sprang up and even the smallest puff was not missed.

"Hoist up all boats!" shouted Hull without leaving the helm.

As soon as the boats came alongside, sailors lifted them up in the light of the battle lanterns. Seamen silently dropped on the deck and laid with half closed eyes, so worn out, they could not even sleep! The Purser Mr. Chew, with bandaged hands, spread out ship biscuits along the deck.

"Here, mate, have some to bring your strength back!" Chew was saying to Seaman Hogan.

"Thankee kindly, Mr. Purser! God bress!" whispered the sailor back, too tired even to notice that Mr. Purser called a common sailor "mate".

Still at the helm, Hull continued giving orders "Mr. Alwyn, set the fore topmast staysail and main topgallant studdingsail!"

Boatswain's pipes called the sailors at the rigging. Tired but still alive, they went up, no complaints were heard. As soon as all sails were set, the thrust moving the frigate forward increased. The working sails sang, merely warming the hearts of the crew with hope that the grueling towing was coming to its end.

"Thank God and our Captain. He got the Constitution's hull scraped thoroughly before going to sea! It might save us!" said Midshipman Greenlaw to Midshipman Gillam.

The Purser overheard and cut in with his usual lecturing voice "Attention to details is VERY important!"

"Like anybody says no. What do you expect, he is the Purser!" whispered Greenlaw to Gillam.

"Turn the glass and strike eight bells!" cried out Alwyn.

The sand hour-glass was inverted marking midnight when Hull turned to Lt. Hoffman "Lt. Hoffman, take this watch. I'll get half an hour of sleep."

The Captain's head dropped on his crossed arms right there on the quarterdeck table next to the binnacle and helm.

"God, send us a real wind! Send us a squall for tomorrow! It is all I am praying for," – the last thought passed thru Captain Hull's mind.

At the sound of the bell tolling once, Hull jumped to his feet. He had so much work to do watching the wind, the current, and the sails that needed constant trimming or setting. His seamanship, his frigate and his skilled crew were all he had, surrounded by five enemy ships...

Nicholas Orloff

♣ ♣ ♣

CHAPTER 15

19th OF JULY 1812. OPEN SEA.
THIS CLOUD WILL BRING US FREEDOM

Timidly, the dark night sky was giving way to dawn with a soft breeze slowly cradling the Constitution. In spite of his sleepless night, Captain Isaac Hull still stayed firmly on the deck, watching the enemy three miles South, with the frigate Aeolus dangerously close - less than a mile Eastward.

"We gained about two miles overnight...." Hull told Lt. Read, then making a decision, "We have to break out of the enemy encirclement. We should get rid of these three frigates surrounding us. Hit them where they are weak... The Aeolus has fewer guns than the others! It is our chance! Change the course to East! Helm – a lee! Off tacks and sheets!"

The Captain was giving the orders, taking the helm. A vein was visibly pulsing at Hull's temple.

In complete silence the Constitution glided close to the Aeolus. The Yankee frigate's tacking was so perfect that the Aeolus missed the opportunity to fire into the ship's stern. Or perhaps the smallest British frigate was waiting to get in closer range to broadside the arrogant ship.

Without any delay, the Aeolus turned and kept a mile behind the Constitution. Dangerously close: a light air puff and the Aeolis could rake her, but at least the Yankee frigate was leaving the enemies behind.

Staying at the helm, Hull shouted "Set my Fore and Main skysails!"

It was the time when he needed them most and the captain was proud of them!

The set skysails caught the wind increasing the humming sound in the sails, boosting the frigate's speed and sailors' spirit.

Three hours later, at 9am, the mast head watch shrieked "Ship ho!"

As if following an order, all heads turned to East in hope to see the squadron hurrying to rescue them. To their disappointment it was a Yankee merchant-ship with an American flag on its mast.

Hull was leaving the helm when Lt. Read cried out "Beg your pardon, Sir, all enemy ships hoisted our flag!"

Hull glanced over his shoulder at enemy. "They bloody lubbers think to catch it as a prize! Hoist the British colors!"

The British flag went up immediately – all war-ships had a set of other countries' flags to decoy an enemy, considered perfectly legal at that time. "Save our souls" – a signal of life and death- none would ever use to lure an enemy or he would be put to shame forever.

The Yankee merchant was no fool – too long had the British used the flag trick. She set all her sails and headed North-East.

"Lookee here, our merchantman is safe! WE saved her!" Seaman Daniel Lewis proudly said to his friend James Frances staying on the mast top.

"We did! See, Dan, the breeze is freshening!" smiled James.

Cheers of excitement spread out on the deck as the humming sound of working sails intensified when the wind increased the ship's speed, bringing hope.

"Mr. Morris, it has been fifty hours since men have slept. Let them have a rest now while it is still possible. Free of the watch can sleep right here on the weather and gun decks. Nobody goes down!" Hull commanded knowing it was far from over yet.

Dead-tired and soaked in sweat, officers and sailors, their faces dirty and unshaven with two days worth of stubble, collapsed onto the decks fast asleep. No rest for Captain Hull though. He was still at the helm trying to catch even the smallest air movement, constantly watching the sails and giving orders to the reefers.

The distance from the enemy ships gradually widened. Cries of joy "We are getting away" broke out over the decks.

At 4 pm the breeze died again, converting the sea surface into a mirror.

"Dunn, take the helm!" Hull shouted to the helmsman.

Once replaced by seamen Richard Dunn, Hull turned to a midshipman. "Mr. Taylor, the lead if you please."

"Aye-aye, sir!"

Waiting for the lead, the Captain stepped to the water bucket, took a big drought, washed his face and neck to cool them off.

"Sir, no bottom with this rope!" Taylor reported, coming running from the ship stern.

"Wake up, Charles, we lost our breeze!" roared Hull to his First Lieutenant, collapsed on the quarterdeck, so tired that the Captain had to shake his shoulder to get him to his senses. "Start towing, too deep for kedging!"

Like a wounded beast, Morris got to his feet "Haul down the boats! Get the tow-line!"

The sailors, leaving their hope for rest behind, rushed to the boats without complaints. The exhausting towing had to be resumed again.

"C'mon, pull harder! We did it so far, we can do it again!" roared the coxswain.

Armed with his old spy-glass, Hull was having an eye on the nearest enemy ship lowering her boats. "Look, Charles, Belvidere hoists out the boats! They bloody ape all we do!"

Always observing the sea and air movement, the Captain suddenly noticed a tiny dark cloud far to South-East. A broad smile lighted up his tired unshaved face with sunken cheeks.

"Mr. Morris, I bet this cloud will bring us freedom!" The Captain pointed.

Officers, all excitement, broke out laughing like madmen. The news spread out along the decks with the speed of lightning.

"Mates, Captain say 'Det cloud'll bring us freedom'!" shouted Seaman James Cheever at the cross-street main mast to the other reefers.

Balancing eighty feet above the deck, Seaman James Ashford uttered "Woo-hoo! Wa-hee! God knows I always hated squalls! But this one... Huzzah, dear squall!"

Sailors at the forecastle watched the cloud, knowing they would have a tough time if the squall hit. Still, they were smiling. One of them, John Brown, cried out "'Tis our sea, it will help us!"

In the full commanding voice to be heard by all hands, the brave Captain shouted "The British imitated all our actions. Make them think a hurricane's coming! Let them think we're scared!"

"Mr. Alwyn, furl the light canvas! Double reef mizzen topsail! Set short sail" Hull passed the orders to Sailing Master and then to the bosun "Mr. Adams, get sailors from the boats aboard. Leave the boats at towing!"

"Mr. Alwyn, make tacks and halyards!" Hull commanded Sailing Master.

Soon a faint air stream lifted the royals. A shrill boatswain's pipe called all towing boats alongside. As soon as they were hooked, the blast stroked the ship. The Constitution heeled to leeward, lifting the boats to the windward clear of the water, sailors skillfully snatching them to the davits.

At the same time the Shannon Sailing Master was shrieking his commands to remove all sails before the storm hit. "Stand by to take in mainsail and spanker! Haul taut! Up mainsail. Lay aloft! Furl mainsail!"

The British sailors spread out along the mainsail. The pressed Nantucket sailor was working on the yard among others. Suddenly he lost the clew – the edge of the sail and dropped the yard. The boatswain shouted at him, spitting with anger. "You, Yankee idiot! I'll send you back to the Guerriere, you stupid dog! Up mainsail, not down! Hurricane's at hands!"

Knowing nobody could see his face from the deck far below, John Dickenson grinned and murmured under his breath "Eat it up, you bloody bastards! Next time think before pressing a Yankee. That was my help for MY country!"

Seamen furl flying jib and jib, balancing on a
thin foot-rope. If a man makes a wrong move, he
fells into the sea-water and will be crashed by
the moving ship. Just imagine staying on
a foot-rope and laying out the upper sails
50-100 feet above the moving deck.

On the Constitution upper deck Hull, a look of excitement in his eyes, was watching the enemy ships as British men climbed aloft, furling absolutely all sails in haste, and abandoning their boats in the sea.

"Ha-ha!" laughed the Yankee Captain, "Look, they believe it's a hurricane. Fools, they don't know our regular Yankee coast squall!"

Finally, the gray cloud, long-awaited, overtook the ship. The rain and fog covered the Constitution, veiling it from the enemy.

"Spread all sails!" Hull hollered.

Cheerful sailors let go the heavy sails - only light canvas were furled before. At once the sails caught the wind multiplying the thrust that sped the Constitution off from her enemies!

Midshipmen Taylor, joy on his face, ran from the stern to Hull. "Sir, fourteen knots!" – 16 miles per hour. It was the fastest speed for frigates at those times...

With revived hope, everybody on the spar-deck - Hull, officers, and seamen laughed, watching the enemy. The Belvidere was cutting ropes and leaving her boats in the sea, eager to chase. Still she was far behind now. Other ships were fishing out their boats, as the squall moved them out for five-ten miles in all directions.

♣ ♣ ♣

CHAPTER 16

20th OF JULY 1812. OPEN SEA.
THE GALLEY STOVE

The rising sun lighted up the enemy sails ten miles west, coloring them cherry-blossom pink. From the Constitution's deck they looked more like tiny spring flowers than menacing warships.

Wearied, dark baggy circles under his eyes, Hull still stood on the quarterdeck like a monument.

"Overnight we gained at least eight miles! Still we must do more! The breeze is too weak. Wet sails kept the wind nicely. Water the sails again!" The Captain ordered to Lt. Hoffman.

"Pump water at sails! Get buckets of water to the tops," piped Boatswain Adams.

Making a live chain on the shrouds, sailors passed buckets of sea-water one to another ninety feet above the rolling deck. Hard and exhausting work, but there were no grimaces, all were smiling.

The main royal, the upper sail on the main mast, was watered by Peter Furnace. The boy had gotten used to the height and started even to like it, feeling as an albatross flying freely above the sparkling sea. Peter's heart sang with joy– he felt useful for the first time after joining the ship's crew!

"Suck it up, ye bloody British! Now ye know Yankee sailors!" Daniel Lewis on the forecastle could not hide his joy. His cry sank in the savage roar came from all the shrouds.

"Lookee, the British give up! They are heading to Sandy Hook! We did it! We won! Huzzah!" Seamen shouted, dancing on the decks. Their mates waved their arms from the mast tops.

"Lt. Hoffman, take this watch, the deck is yours. Course North-North East! Since we can not get to New York, we will be heading to Boston instead. Wake me up if you see any sail. I am turning in. Let people off duty have some sleep."

A bright smile shone on Hull's tired face. "They did it! Somehow they did it! His new crew did it! Unbelievable," passed thru the Captain's mind.

"And Lt. Hoffman, pass the word to Mr. Alwyn to start the galley-stove. Tell the cook to make a good hot dinner for all hands!" The Captain paused recollecting, "oh, no time to soak the salted beef? Tell Stone to provide ham, potatoes and beer from my private pantry for the crew!"

"Aye, Aye, sir!" Lt. Hoffman saluted. His teeth flushed foreseeing a feast.

At four in the afternoon, not able to wait until dinner was ready, a group of seamen gathered around the stove, the kingdom of Old Jack. Busy as a huge fat bee, the old seaman was cooking, smiling widely. The heat of the galley-stove fire combined with the hot afternoon did not spoil Old Jack's high spirits. He even hummed a tune while simmering something in huge pots fixed on hooks above burning wood.

Still asleep, Seaman John Brown sniffed the air like a fox and, following the smell, walked to the stove, his eyes still shut.

"Smells like heaven!" he said, opening one eye. "What is det, Old Jack?"

Laughing with delight, the cook Jack waved his big wooden spoon. "My dear lads, today we are havin' a royal stew: our Captain provided ham, onions, potatoes and a barrel of beer from his PRIVATE pantry! I added beans and beer into the stew! 'course beer can not spoil any dish! It IS BEER! Ha-ha!"

Seaman George Reynolds lifted his eyes to the sky "Thank ye, God! Thank ye! What a lucky day! First we escaped de British and now be given de stew! I'm so hungry; I could eat a rat alive if I could catch one."

His mate Hogan cut in "Bress my soul, mates, I dought we were busted! Do be surrounded by four frigates and de Two-Decker!"

"Me too! We, says I, were less than half a mile from de enemy without wind!" John Brown said feeling his stomach twisted with hunger.

"Gor bress de Captain! What courage!" Hogan could not stop but saying.

"What seamanship! He did not miss even the smallest air puff! So many hours at the helm," exclaimed Reynolds.

Old Jack wiped wet hands on his apron, took a spoon of the stew and passed it to seamen to taste – an unusual gesture for the cook. "Salt enough?"

Hogan eagerly took the spoon savoring the stew in his turn "Joosy, berry joosy!"

"Say what ye will, brothers, ain't Captain Hull the best captain in the Navy! He made the whole crew work together as one single man! Even the Purser went into the blue cutter and oared as a jack tar! Ain't ye see his hands? All his skin has gone!" Old Jack continued.

"Ye said true! And de midshipmen manning de capstan bars! Never heard before of a ship where officers respect foremast jacks. Bress my soul, it's due to our Captain!" John Brown said.

"Hull is the bravest captain I ever sailed with! Have ye heard how he saved his Captain from drowning when he was just sixteen?" Squeaking John's voice was heard.

"And how he captured the French privateer "Sandwich" in 1800?" cut in his friend Caleb Smith, "Tomahawk".

Seaman Hogan could hardly wait for his turn "Upon my soul, I am about of de same opinion! With such a captain I'm ready to fight all the British Navy!"

All seamen shouted "Damn, right! Listen to him!"

♣ ♣ ♣

CHAPTER 17

JULY 26th 1812. BOSTON.
THE SITUATION IS HOPELESS

As soon as the Constitution dropped anchor in Boston, Lt. John Shubrick was sent to New York with the utmost dispatch to check the Admiralty and Commodore Rogers' orders.

Hull wanted to have the frigate ready to sail once orders were received: food provisions, powder and 20000 gallons of fresh water had to be taken in.

It was wearing work to stack hundreds of heavy barrels into the frigate's lowest deck, where they acted as ballast to keep the ship upright. If not done correctly, the cargo would move on the high seas, overturning the ship and bringing death to the sailors.

Listening to the sounds of the big city and catching an occasional glimpse of the women passing by was all the joy seamen could allow themselves, working hard loading the large water-barrels. The Constitution crew was perfectly aware that their ship was one of the three heavy frigates the young country could rely upon.

Forgetting about going ashore, seamen wondered where the squadron was and how Rogers could let the British sail freely under his nose.

By Navy regulations, first thing at a port, the ship-captain had to report to the port-admiral right there in the harbor. Hull found the door locked, the big boss being out of Boston visiting his sick relative and was not expected back soon. It seemed nobody really cared – a usually busy harbor went dead - most merchant ships were captured and taken away by the English. The others stayed in Boston to avoid being caught. Only small fishing boats dared to sail nearby - the British would not bother catching them.

Not having found the port-admiral, Hull headed to the Exchange Coffee-House just a few steps off the harbor on State Street – an eight storied building, the highest in Boston and the famous gathering point where Bostonians met and discussed the news.

Having opened the door, the captain was surprised: dreary atmosphere, hushed conversations, no usual jokes to be heard, just gloom as if a spider's web was hanging about.

"All trade is dead." Hull heard a man saying sadly.

Another one added with despair "And our fleet! Just a handful of warships against the British thousand, highly trained!"

Captain Hull took a step in. A man next to the entrance turned his head to the newcomer. Recognizing Hull, he jumped to his feet to greet the Captain, his face all surprise and admiration. "Captain Hull from the Constitution! Good day to you, Sir!"

All conversation at the tables stopped immediately. Everybody rushed towards Hull, eager to hear the news.

"Captain Hull, is it true the entire British squadron tried to capture the Constitution just off the New Jersey coast?"

Hull grinned "Not quite. Not the entire British squadron. It was ship-of-the-line Africa, frigates Shannon, Guerriere, Belvidere, and Aeolis along with a brig and a schooner... Quite a company though!"

"And the Constitution was all by herself?" a voice was heard.

"How close were the British?" cut in another one.

"Yes, just the Constitution. We were near to being caught, especially with no wind at all. Due to the crew's great efforts we managed to escape."

"Gosh! Five ships with the flagman Shannon and the famous Guerriere failed to capture a single frigate?! Tell us more!" all the coffee-house guests shouted as one.

"I will, but first give me the news. Where is our squadron?"

"Sailed to the English Channel right after the war was declared..." Deep mortification sounded in the man's voice.

"...making our merchants easy prey for the British!" Other Bostonians added.

"The frigate Guerriere robs our inshore villages! They feel our land belongs to them!" echoed the third one.

"What about our army?" The Constitution's Captain asked.

"Not good. They sent your uncle, General William Hull, to Detroit with just a thousand untrained men," an old Bostonian in a black coat answered, anger showing in his voice.

"...against regular British troops and the local Indians the British cleverly set against us." Another one finished the thought.

"The situation is hopeless!" all cried out.

Hull frowned, never expecting to hear anything worse.

A tall man from the table next to the window bowed "Captain Hull, I am afraid, there is bad news for you. I've just come from New York. Begging your pardon but I heard your younger brother William is seriously ill."

Even an enemy cutlass could not hurt Hull as painfully as this news...

"My little brother! The closest friend of my childhood... He is just thirty five. What about his wife and the children, if, God forbid, he dies..." The captain thought, hurrying back to his ship.

♣ ♣ ♣

CHAPTER 18

August 1 1812. BOSTON. TOUGH DECISION

Three days of hard labor passed in a blink of an eye and the sailors sat at the mess table having two evening hours to themselves. Under a dimly lit lamp they were listening to jack tar Asa Curtis read the last issue of "Niles Weekly Register".

"Captain Hull, finding his friends in Boston are correctly informed of his situation when chased by the British squadron off New York, and that they are good enough to give him more credit for having escaped them than he ought to claim, takes this opportunity of requesting them to make a great part of their good wishes to Lieutenant Morris, and the other brave officers, and the crew under his command, for their many great-exertions and prompt attention to orders while the enemy were in chase."

"Read further, mate!" Squeaking John asked eagerly.
"Captain Hull has great pleasure in saying, that notwithstanding the length of the chase, and the officers and crew being deprived of sleep, and allowed but little refreshment during the time, not a murmur was heard to escape them." Asa Curtis lifted his head and looked around with triumph.

"The Captain ain't say much of himself. If not him, we would not have made it." Cut in Daniel Lewis, his usually ugly scar looking like a second smile.

Seamen at the table and those sitting nearby shouted "True, indeed! Listen to him!"

"My chap, will you be so good as to copy dis for me, will you? Dere is a piece of paper. I'll send it to my parents. Dey'll be proud!" James Ashford asked.

"And for me too, mate!" Many voices joined.

The sailors, being proud of what they read about themselves in the paper, rushed along the decks spreading the news among the others who had not heard it yet. Even the captain in the Great Cabin could hear their muffled excited exclamations "There! In the paper! About us! Can you believe it?!"

A quick knock on the door and Lt. John Shubrick, the messenger back from New York, burst into the Great Cabin.

"Sir, according to your orders... with the utmost dispatch... just from New York... no packages, no letters left for you by Commodore Rodgers," reported Shubrick, hardly catching his breath.

"Anything from the Admiralty?"

"No, sir, not today!"

"Thank, you, Lieutenant!"

Shubrick saluted, leaving the Cabin and Hull alone with his thoughts.

"What am I to do? No new orders. The previous were to join Rogers in New York."

The Captain opened the envelope, unfolded the paper with his orders from July 3rd and read attentively what he had already memorized word by word:

"...As soon as the Constitution is ready for sea, you will weigh anchor and proceed to New York.

...If, on your way thither, you should fall in with an enemy's vessel, you will be guided in your proceeding by your own judgment, bearing in mind, however, that you are not voluntarily to encounter a force superior to your own.

On your arrival at New York, you will report yourself to Commodore Rodgers. If he should not be in that port, you will remain there until further orders."

Hull lifted his head thinking "The squadron is in the English Channel, in the best case it will be back in two months. Could be six months easily! What am I to do?"

The captain stood up and drew near the stern window, his mind racing "Should I stay in Boston being just a gun battery? Who will defend our merchants? Who will stop the British delivering the supplies for their army? It's time to act!"

The ship's bell on the spar-deck tolled six. Hull listened until its last sound died away. "Nevertheless, I should not sail without orders..."

A talk between First Lt. Morris and the Sailing Master Alwyn - the quarterdeck with air hatch being right above Hull's head - caught Captain's attention.

"Lieutenant Morris, we have just finished loading water-barrels."

"Very good, Mr. Alwyn. We are now ready to sail off."

"Charles, when do you think we put to sea? Have the new orders arrived?"

"Not that I heard of."

"What a waste! After our miraculous escape all hands believe the Constitution can do anything. The fighting spirit will be gone if we stay in Boston longer."

"Indeed, it will. On the other hand, you are aware of the consequences should we sail without orders. If, God forbid, the British capture us? The Captain will be hung from a yardarm."

"Damn, to that!" Hull forced himself to stop listening further. "All I know I have to defend my country. Nothing is more important!"

Hull knew that orders were issued by the secretary of the Admiralty who was far from being a sailor himself. Being reluctant to lose a ship, the Secretary Hamilton would not risk a single frigate sail while the British squadron roamed nearby. Hamilton could not even understand that the miraculous escape of the Constitution multiplied her chances of defeating a British ship of her class.

"I know with such a crew we can win one on one. If, God forbid, we meet the British squadron? ...Well, we escaped once; we can do it again!" Hull kept thinking.

The ship's bell above his head stroked seven. A deep sigh escaped Hull's chest "My dear brother... What if he died while I am at sea?"

The thought of losing his younger brother pierced Hull. He gasped heavily and buried his face in his hands...

A long moment passed before the Captain could collect himself.

"I am an officer of the United States Navy and it is war time. My duty is to lead the ship."

Hull had finally made up his mind when a polite knock at the door caught his attention.

"Beg your pardon, Sir!" Morris saluted his Captain. "A fisherman said he saw the British frigate Maidstone lurking off Cape Cod just two days ago."

"This is it. Charles, we'll sail at the morning tide. No time to lose!"

Nicholas Orloff

♣ ♣ ♣

CHAPTER 19

AUGUST 19ᵗʰ 1812.
JUST A BUNCH OF CONVICTS

On a rainy and cloudy afternoon the Constitution was steering South-South West, fresh breeze in her sails. The Captain and the First Lieutenant were planning a new drill in a couple of minutes.

Two weeks ago the brave Yankee frigate sailed off North of Boston Lighthouse to the British blockade station at Nova Scotia, looking for enemy ships. A fortnight and not a single minute lost: drill held every day to get sailors ready for battle. Once the exercise was finished, the sailors had to sew iron-strapped canvas protection caps for the boarding party. The caps would also help to differentiate a Yankee from an enemy during the battle. A huge heap of sponges and wads was prepared by the Master Gunner's mates. The tuff-rail, damaged during their escape from the British, was newly repaired. Sharpened cutlasses, pikes, and boarding axes glittered under the sun. But that was not all - during those two weeks the Constitution was chasing, and putting fire to enemy armed brigs and merchants, setting Yankee ships free.

Some would have been satisfied, but not Captain Hull. He was looking forward to meeting an English frigate – a ship of their class.

Hull learned from captured British sailors and freed Yankee merchants that the enemy frigates Belvidera, Guerriere, Shannon, Spartan, Pomone, Aeolis, and two-decker Africa cruised nearby with orders to take or burn any Yankee ship they met...

"...Well, two weeks at sea and no enemy frigates in sight so far... Where the hell are they hiding?" Hull hardly finished his words when the mast head cry split apart the afternoon. "On deck there! Sail-ho! Hull down!"

The old telescope immediately focused on a frigate the same size as the Constitution steering East by South.

"Here she comes!" Hull passed the telescope to Morris.

Half an hour later, Hull chuckled. "What a pleasant surprise, it's the Guerriere, that chased us! Get men on the deck, I have to talk to them!"

The sound of Boatswain Adams' pipes to muster had not yet died as sailors gathered on the spar deck having left the hatches.

"Shipmates! Remember our chasers? It's one of them, the Guerriere, of our class. Now we are at even odds... So shall we go home?" The captain grinned, perfectly aware of the high spirits of his crew.

Seamen burst out laughing, and then roared "No! Let's show them, pompous cockroaches! Let's fight for our land! Huzzah!"

Hull smiled; he did not expect a better reply.

"So, with your permission, we will see today if the Guerriere can fight one on one," said Hull and then shouted, lifting his hand, "For those who died on the Chesapeake! For our Constitution!"

Sailors' cheers followed the captains words "For the Chesapeake! For our Constitution! Just get us alongside! Huzzah!"

"All hands about ship! Set all sails. Course East by South," ordered Hull not missing a second.

It took less than a quarter of an hour to have in place all the sails the frigate could bear to speed off the Yankee ship towards the enemy.

At 3:35 pm Hull, watching the Guerrierre, which in French means Warrior, noticed that she backed her Main topsail – to an experienced eye it meant the enemy was getting ready for battle, sure to win.

The Yankee captain ordered take in the light sails, set down Royal Yards, reef in the topsails, haul up foresail and mainsail. Sailors hurried up to execute fearlessly, even though not many of them had ever been in a battle before. All looked excited about the fight to come.

Young Peter Furnace worked on the Main Royal Yard –always manned by boys – the weight of an adult being too heavy for the delicate upper mast that held the highest sail of the ship.

Peter felt the royal mast swaying, the stays–ropes supporting the mast tightened like fiddle strings, onduring the tension of the yard filled with a fresh breeze. The boy heard the sail's high pitch hum, followed by the deep bass of the large yards below.

The wind freshened, blowing away heavy clouds and a glimpse of the sun peeked thru, glistening on the sea-surface.

Peter's heart filled with joy – it had been a month since he had first climbed up to the rigging. Just one month, and the fear of heights was conquered.

"Today I would see a real battle! The boys of my neighborhood would die of envy! What a stroke of luck!" The powder-boy thought climbing down to the deck when a new order came from the captain: "Beat to quarters!"

Soon guns replaced clothes drying out on the long line and a checker game was swept away from the mess-table, the table itself moved to the orlop. The gully-fire put out – hot coals went overboard. The perfectly clean and shiny deck floor was covered with sand. Slow matches fumed from the sand-buckets. Boarding axes, cutlasses stored next to the hammocks nettings. All the battle-stations were taken. Thirty-two pound smashers and long guns ran-out of the open ports.

The carronade under the gun captain Squeaking John's command, the nearest to the quarterdeck, was directed ominously at the approaching enemy. John's friend, Caleb Smith "Tomahawk", a boarder in the gun's crew, hugged Squeaking John "It is our day, my friend, d'ye hear? Just get me close to board and my tomahawk will crash enemy scalps! Today we'll show these bloody dogs what a Yankee frigate is worth! We are not bad ourselves!"

"And a Yankee carronade!" Squeaking John kissed his carronade. "Take care, brother! God bress!"

"God keep you safe!"

...Exactly at that time Captain Dacres on the Guerriere quarter-deck was carefully watching the strange sail.

"What kind of ship is it? I can not make it out." Dacres asked his First Lieutenant.

"Not sure, sir," the First Lieutenant shook his head. "Is it one of ours? An American would not dare!"

"Bring Captain Orne here, the prisoner from the Boston brig Betsey," Dacres ordered to his midshipman, a boy of twelve.

The merchant brig Betsey was taken by the Guerierre a couple of days before. Since then its crew was locked up in the frigate's hold along with other Yankee prisoners.

Narrowing his eyes to protect them from the blazing sun which seemed even brighter after the hold's darkness, the captain-prisoner stepped on the quarterdeck, wondering why he was called up.

"Captain Orne, what do you make of that ship?" Dacres asked without a greeting.

Orne looked at the Constitution "A Yankee frigate, all right."

His words sounded like music to Dacres's ears.

"Coming too boldly for a bunch of pine boards!" The British captain laughed with delight "Run our colors!"

A couple of minutes later the bosun's pipe signaled "Word to be passed" and all the sailors knew it called for silence - an important order would follow. Indeed, covering the sea-noise Dacres cried out thru a trumpet "Guerrieres, here comes a Yankee frigate. In forty-five minutes she is ours. Take her in fifteen and I promise you four months pay!"

"Huzzah to four months pay!" Seamen shouted at the happy news.

"Get a bucket of molasses and rum on deck to sweeten his Majesty's victory!" Dacres commanded, laughing merrily.

"Sailing Master, make topsails and jib! Get the wind on the starboard quarter to take advantage of the wind! Let the Yankee see British seamanship," exclaimed the English captain, so sure of himself and his crew.

"Boatswain, let the pressed American sailors stay in the hold if they don't wish to fight against their countrymen!" It was noble of the British captain: ten pressed Yankee sailors manned the British frigate's crew.

"Aye, Sir," saluted the boatswain, although in a minute he winked to his First mate "Those Yankee lubbers will fight as others, we don't have spare hands! The more get shot, the better! I don't give a damn!"

With set sails, the Guerriere maneuvered skillfully when the next command followed "Clear the ship for action!"

Goats, chicken coops, the barrels of provisions had to be moved into the orlop. One of the pressed sailors, John Dickenson, grabbed a chicken coop and dropped it, pretending he had slipped. Cackling in panic, two red hens ran back and forth along the gun deck getting in sailors' way. Dickenson followed as he was chasing the birds but in fact adding to the mess, knocking down the seamen unfastening the long guns tackles at the bulwark. The boatswain shouted at him, spitting angrily "You, clumsy Yankee idiot! I'll show you!"

...Dacres commanded "Cast loose your guns! Marines, up to the mast head!"

Red jackets rushed up immediately and set, ready for shooting.

"Master at Arms, lock the prisoner in the hold!"

As Captain Orne went down, led by the Master at Arms, he saw the British ready at their guns, a blood thirsty look on their faces.

The pressed Yankee sailor Dickenson nodded to him, the only friendly face among the herd of the enemies.

"The third prize in five days!" Orne heard the British seamen saying to each other. "A frigate! At least three months pay! What a lucky day! Ha-ha."

"The Yankees ain't no seaman! Just a bunch of bastards and outlaws! They'd better hide in their harbors and not peek out!" The British boatswain said brashly.

Having noticed that anger darkened Yankee captain's face, the Master at Arms tapped him on a shoulder laughing. "Cheer up, Yankee! In thirty minutes you'll have plenty of company from your frigate!"

The door slammed behind Orne's back and was locked as soon as he stepped into the hold. Minutes passed before the Yankee merchant captain could distinguish anything in a dim light of a thin candle inside an old dusty lamp. Another ten prisoners in the hold, a small, cramped dark space below the water-line, surrounded Orne, eager to hear the news.

"Captain, what's up there?" one of the prisoners asked.

"Yankee frigate, Constitution, I believe."

"All by herself? Will the Guerriere catch it?" the second voice cut in.

"Sir, is there any hope for her to flee?" Teenager Elijah Adams questioned politely. The boy was taken as a hostage from a Yankee merchant ship just hours before. His father, Captain Adams had to sail to Boston to collect five thousand dollars as a ransom to free his son.

"Hm...To tell you the truth, I don't know what to think of it. The Yankee frigate is coming straight at us. Can't make out what their thinking is."

"Could our frigate fight the Guerriere?" Elijah Adams still had hope.

"Nah, you silly head, it is suicide. The British are kings at sea! No one: not French, not Spaniards, not Dutch can fight them..." the first voice explained to the boy.

"All we can do is to pray for our frigate!" Captain Orne said sitting down on the floor and starting "Our Father" joined by the others.

♣ ♣ ♣

CHAPTER 20

AUGUST 19th 1812. OPEN SEA. OLD IRON-SIDES

A thousand yards separated the frigates at five in the afternoon when the Guerriere fired the first broadside. All her starboard (the right side) guns sounded in unison which would have made the Admiral Nelson proud. The Guerriere went straight at the enemy, as the legendary British admiral taught. However, all her 18-pound balls fell short – the first firing was meant for aiming, so the next one would be corrected and go home.

As a perfect example of British Naval tactics, the Guerriere skillfully tackled and gave a larboard (the left side) broadside, not eight minutes had passed. Most balls flew above the Constitution but one struck the larboard knighthead, sending long splinters all around.

"God damn good gunnery," flashed thru Hull's mind when another ball hit the foremast, cutting the hoop in two.

The splinter-netting spread above the spar-deck caught many sharp oak splinters but some pierced several seamen, killing Robert Bruce. A two foot long piece of wood hit Caleb Smith's chest, putting down the boarder in the crew nearest to the quarterdeck smasher. Replacing his fallen mate, the carronade's sponger, James Cheever, picked up the gun side tackle.

With a shriek "Caleb" Squeaking John dropped on his knees next to his friend and drew out the splinter. Pressing the wound with his fingers, John lifted Caleb's head and held it against his chest. Tomahawk, who saved John's life many years back when his bowels were pumping out of his cut-open belly, murmured with already colorless lips "My time, mate!"

"No, Caleb, no! Don't you die on me!" John shouted.

"Make the British swabs pay! Fight for both of us..." Caleb stopped breathing; and his body went limp.

"We will show them, bastards! Ye have my word!" Squeaking John kissed his friend's forehead, and then bent over the carronade muzzle shouting "For our Constitution! And for you, Caleb!"

Firing occasionally, Guerriere maneuvered, adjusting to a position that would allow her to rake the Yankee frigate from the stern to the bow, cutting all her masts in one broadside.

Nevertheless, all Dacres' efforts were in vain: after three quarters of an hour of trying, the English captain realized that Constitution was his match in the seamanship. Striving forward to bring the wind on her starboard quarter, the Guerriere fired her guns with her side directed to the Yankee.

A loud cheer spread out on the British decks at the sight of the ball that had cut the Constitution rigging and sent up a cloud of splinters.

"Why don't they fire? And can they, Yankee, fire at all? Ha-Ha" seamen laughed.

"Just a bunch of convicts! What d'ey know?" another one giggled.

"We have been mastering guns for years!" a midshipman joined them.

At that very time a new command sounded on the Constitution quarterdeck. "Mr. Morris, get me alongside – we have them outgunned but with this new crew we need to close-in! Then the Yankee gun power will be revealed!" shouted Hull. "Spread Main topgallant and foresail!" Once the sails were set, the distance between the ships began decreasing fast.

Squeaking John saluted Lt. Morris "Sir, can we fire now?"

"Wait" Lt. Morris ran to the quarterdeck, "Sir, Two of our men killed. Shall we open fire?"

"Not yet, sir. Courage now!" Hull shouted so that all hands could hear him.

"Get closer!" Hull commanded the helmsman.

"Aye, closer it is!" The helmsman Dunn confirmed.

Heading straight at his enemy, Hull was altering course giving the Guerriere's gunners a hard time aiming.

"Change course two points to larboard! Mr. Alwyn, keep to the British stern! We must avoid her broadsides! When within a pistol shot, get me alongside!"

"Permission to fire, sir?" Squeaking John eagerly asked Morris.

"Wait!" Morris shook his head "Captain wants to get closer, to have all shots go home. Courage now!"

"Change course two points to starboard" another order from the captain disturbed the enemy's aim.

A couple of minutes later, not able to wait longer, Lt. Morris, ran to the Captain's side again "Sir, shall we open fire? Less than half a mile already!"

"No, wait! Get marines on the maintop!"

Blue jackets of the American marines rushed up with muskets, and set ready to shoot. The frigates were so close that Yankee sailors could see their enemy's faces clearly. They even could see their eyes sparkling with hatred!

"Haul down the jib! Trim main topsail" - the captain wanted the Constitution to slow down, ready to broadside.

"Sir, shall we open fire? The tension is unbearable!" Morris begged.

"No, don't waste the first volley! Wait," barked Hull. "So much for well-drilled crew! They even could not wait for a command!" passed thru his mind.

Hull knew that after firing so many times the English guns had become too hot and needed time to cool down. It would give him a chance to get a closer position without the risk of getting shot. On the other hand, his guns were ready to drop all seven hundred pounds of metal, the Constitution's full broadside.

In a minute, the Yankee ship was alongside the Guierriere. But it seemed an eternity for seaman - so eager they were to start firing.

Just a pistol shot's distance separated the ships with the English starboard side to the Constitution, when Hull roared "Now! Hull her! On the up-roll! Aim at the masts! Fire!"

These words sounded like a blessing to Yankee seamen. A split second and Squeaking John's slow match ignited the smasher's vent. The carronade fired and the 32 pound ball hissed in the thick cloud of smoke joining the thunderous roar of eleven carronades on the spar-deck and fifteen 24-pounder long guns on the gun-deck.

With deafening noise Yankee iron balls crashed thru the Guirierre's timbers sending splinters and torn-out iron rigging blocks all over the English deck.

Bloody mess everywhere. Some British sailors were wounded. Others were not able to join the Creator, being torn down to pieces, creating an Apocalypse picture printed in blood...

His Majesty's gun-crews were not used to such treatment from the enemy. Discouraged, they fired in haste as soon as their guns were primed without proper aiming, sending shots too high.

The pressed Nantucket sailor John Dickenson put a slow match down before handing it to the gun-captain. A shout "You idiot, get another one," sounded like music to John.

...On the other ship the Yankee worked as robots, reloading fast but took the time to range their gun-sights on enemy's hull or spar.

"Sponge!" Squeaking John cried out.

In a wink James Cheever, the sponger, cleaned the muzzle with lamb-wool on a spike, turning it three times right, and three times left, to be sure no powder was left in the barrel. Otherwise the gun barrel would blow to pieces when an iron ball or a powder bag was being inserted.

"Prime- Point your gun," came from Morris.

Squeaking John crouched over his smasher and looked along it's barrel, aiming at the Guerriere's mizzen mast.

"Fire!"

A 32-pound ball sent from Squeaking John's carronade flew straight at the Guerriere's mizzen-mast, crashing the rail on the starboard side. With a pitching sound the mizzen went overboard.

A wild cheer from the Constitution covered the roar of cannons and carronades.

"Get it, you bloody rascals! This is for Caleb Smith!" Squeaking John hollered, dancing around his smasher.

Having snatched off his hat, Hull waved it, shouting "Hurrah, Constitutions! We made a brig of her! Make a sloop!"

Still firing, the Constitution's crew cracked with laughter – for each seaman knows a brig has two masts and a sloop just one.

Excited, Hull was jumping up until he split his breeches. No time to change though, the captain commanded the ship.

...Back to the Guerriere. Frightened by the tremendous bump of an explosion that jolted the hull, making the ship reel and tremble, young Elijah Adams asked, startled by the noise "God, what was that?"

"Ha-ha! Even if we are sinking, it is the best sound I could hope for! Looks like a Yankee's ball smashed a mast or made a hole in our hull," laughed Captain Orne.

The other prisoners joined "Huzzah! Huzzah, Constitution!"

The prisoners stopped abruptly when they heard the British began cheering as madman. They did not know that an English ball hit the Constitution's fore royal truck, and shot away two halyards, one with the fifteen star flag. According to a sea law, a flag down meant surrender.

...In a blink of an eye Yankee Irish-born seaman Daniel Hogan rushed to the fallen flag. After lifting it from the Constitution's deck, the sailor went up into the topmast rigging.

Cannon balls were hissing above his head. The marines on the Guierriere's topmast aimed their muskets at Hogan.

Forgetting about the danger, the brave sailor kept climbing up. All sounds muffled, he moved further as in a dream. Just the flag and the mast were real. "I've got to do it, I've got to!" These words flashed thru Hogan's head. Reaching the top, he bound the fifteen star flag to the topmast, and then sped down, letting the shroud between his bent legs, cheered by his mates.

A minute later John Brown witnessed a British 18-pound ball hit the Constitution's hull, made a dent, and fell into the water. Amazed, the old jack tar shouted "Lookoo horo! English ball couldn't bond our hull! Huzzah! Constitution's sides are made of iron!"

At these words, Peter Furnace started dancing, overwhelmed by joy.

"She is made of iron! Our dear Old Iron-sides!" the cries spread out fore and aft giving a birth to the nick-name written in annals of history.

In 1812 no ships were made of iron. However, the Constitution's creator Joshua Humphreys, implementing Washington's decision to build six frigates to protect America "from insult or aggression" and knowing the young country could not match the Britain in number of ships-of-war, had a vision to design a fast-sailing frigate with a solid hull capable of escaping English ships-of-the line.

Joshua suggested a long keel (under-water length) with a narrow beam (width) and diagonal riders at hull-frame similar to the Pennsylvania Dutch barn roofs. It was thought a ship riders had to be spaced two or three feet apart. Joshua suggested having less than two inch gaps between the riders, packed with crushed rock salt to preserve the wood. It created a solid wall almost two feet thick. That was how the Constitution hull was built! The strongest, long lasting lumber of white pine, white oak and southern live oak was used for framing.

She surely could carry thirty 24-pound long guns weighting three tons each! Two hundred years passed and still engineers applaud the young ship-builder from Philadelphia, wondering how he could imagine the Constitution building plan of that complexity without any computers and test labs... A pencil, a ruler, a blank paper and a genius head - was all that it took.

♣ ♣ ♣

CHAPTER 21

AUGUST 19th 1812. OPEN SEA.
I HAVE... TO SURRENDER

The mizzen mast, still held by its rigging, acted as an anchor that suddenly brought the Guierriere around across the wind. The Constitution shot ahead of her.

"Helm hard to Port!" ordered Hull to Dunn-the helmsman, to force the enemy frigate to steer into the same direction or risk being raked from the Constitution's larboard battery.

"Port hard it is!" Dunn repeated the given course – this was required by the Navy regulations - then turned the helm left.

As Hull had foreseen, the Guierriere undertook tackling to port. It failed though, dragged by the mizzen in water.

Hull took his chance. "Rake her!"

Broadside after broadside, the Yankee frigate was pouring iron into the enemy. A sudden strong gust sent the Constitution gliding before the wind. Thanking God for his luck, the Guerriere's Captain attempted to flee, turning to starboard. Even without a mast, the British frigate still had chance to escape.

In a blink of an eye, the skillful Yankees, determined to win, turned to the starboard intercepting the enemy. Soon the Constitution lay alongside the Guerriere again, firing her guns. It was then that the English ship, being without her mast, lost control and sent the bowsprit over the Constitution's stern, straight at the mizzen rigging.

The Guerriere's figurehead was so close that John Brown leaned out of the Great Cabin's open port and touched it. "Just ye wait, ye bloody dog!" Brown said, turning his back to the enemy hull, and continued sponging his long gun.

The Guerriere's bowsprit above the Constitution's spar deck provided a chance to board. Not a moment to lose, Lt. Morris rushed to the Guerriere's bowsprit to lash its ropes, thus preventing the enemy ship's movement. Risky business - the English mast heads muskets took aim at the brave officer who kept fixing the bowsprit rigging with rope, challenging death.

Not waiting for orders, James Frances and Daniel Lewis hurried to Lt. Morris's side. Having fought many battles, the old friends knew a single second could win an action.

Working hard, Lewis caught sight of a British pistol pointed at his friend James. With the pistol being at point blank, there was no time to take shelter. Without a second thought Daniel leapt forward, shielding his sworn black brother.

Ripping thru the seaman's shirt, the deadly bullet pierced Lewis's chest. The saved black seaman grabbed Daniel and dragged his limp body to the sick-berth where six men with dressed wounds huddled on the floor in semidarkness. Two, with more serious wounds, occupied hammocks.

"O-o-o, ye bloody skunks!" Pale with blood loss, captain's servant Ivan Stone was groaning. "How will the captain do without me?"

A stained bandage covered Stone's one eye and forehead. His other eye though did not fail to notice the newcomers. "What's new up there, mate?"

"Our boarding axes ready!" dropped Frances making his way thru the wounded.

Begging surgeon Evans to take care of his best friend, Frances sat on a bare floor with Daniel in his lap.

The surgeon, all but his face smeared with blood, stood over an operation table, making the last stitches on a man struck with a splinter. The patient was gritting his teeth overcoming pain "Ye, English bilge rats, I'll show ye one day! O-o-o! Ye, English gasbags, screw ye!" Then recollecting that no swearing allowed on the frigate, he murmured "Begging your pardon, Mr. Surgeon!"

"That's ok," smiled the surgeon.

As soon as Evans finished, his two mates moved the wounded man to a small cot and handed him a mug "Have some grog, mate! You did well!"

Frances did not waste a second. With a surgeon mate's help, he placed his friend on an operating table. In a heart beat a rope tightened up Lewis's arms and legs to the table to prevent movement during the surgery. Grog replaced anesthesia.

No time even for a drought of water - a new patient was waiting. Taking a deep breath, Evans only managed to wipe off his sweating face with the back of his arm that smeared his forehead with fresh blood.

After cutting Lewis's shirt and making an incision, the surgeon separated the edges of the wound with an old retractor, used on another wounded man just minutes before.

In the dim light of the sick-berth lanterns hanging above the sea chests that served as an operating table, the surgeon dug into the flesh, looking for the bullet.

Either due to Evans's skills or Lewis's good fortune: the bullet with the small piece of Daniel's shirt it took while piercing the body, was reached soon.

"Check if this patches the hole on the shirt,"told the surgeon his mate Donaldson Yeates.

Yeates placed the dug out piece of material soaked with blood to the shirt "Aye, sir, patches nicely!"

Evans grinned "Mate, you're in luck today, your rib stopped the bullet before it could reach the right lung," and began sewing the wound up.

Soon the wounded was moved into a cot.

"Thank you, brother! You saved my life!" The black sailor said, holding his friend's hand.

Despite the pain, Lewis smiled with colorless lips. "Paid back... ye saved me from Hell-ship," whispered Daniel Lewis...

The black sailor tapped Lewis on his shoulder "Have a good rest now, I have to go."

"Take care of the Captain, mate!" Stone begged.

"Show those stinky rats," cried out the wounded.

"We'll show them!" James Frances hustled up to the weather deck to continue the battle, just in time as the Captain shouted "Boarders away!"

Wearing protective iron-strapped canvas caps, sailors with boarding axes – tomahawks and cutlasses ran to the Guerriere's bowsprit. Ahead of all was First Lt. of Marines William Bush, leading the Yankee boarders. He leapt to the tuff-rail but immediately fell down motionless, with a gun-shot wound in what used to be his face and now looked a bloody mess.

Officer's golden epaulettes attracted the English muskets and pistols like a magnet. Still, Lt. Morris took over "Yankees, follow me!"

The First Lieutenant jumped on tuff-rail and in no time a musket ball found him, passing thru his abdomen. Morris bent trying to keep his balance and stay on the rail, but fainted dropping motionless.

"Get Mr. Morris down!" shouted Alwyn.

... When sailors lifted the First Lieutenant's feeble body, blood streamed from his abdomen, leaving a red track behind. Coming back to his senses, Morris tried to press the wound but blood still was pulsing thru his fingers.

In his turn, the Sailing Master Alwyn leaped to tuff-rail "For our Constitution! Follow me!"

Blink of an eye and a bullet tore a piece of his epaulette and ripped flesh, opening a white bone. For a minute, Alwyn, still on tuff-rail, moved back and forth, and then fell down. Trying to get on his feet, the Sailing Master gripped the ship's side, smearing it red - his coat sleeve was soaked with blood.

At this moment Captain Hull decided it was his turn to lead the boarders and headed to the tuff-rail. Immediately all English muskets took their aim, recognizing a captain's uniform.

In a split second Seaman James Ashford appeared at Hull's side and dragged him down from tuff-rail without ceremony pointing out captain's gold epaulets.

"Sir, ain't go with those swabs on!" Ashford cried sheltering Hull from musket balls flying like a swarm of bees, each carrying death.

One ball hit James. The gallant seaman fell at the feet of his captain, but Hull was safe!

Having bent over Ashford, the captain watched the dying seaman smile "Show them!"

"God be with you! Thank you, mate" Hull said, "Get Ashford down!"

The Seamen's body was lifted and carried below—nobody, not even the dead, went overboard on the Constitution during the battle.

"Boarders, back off! We rake her until she strikes! Lt. Read, keep firing! We have to save our people! Double shots with round and grape!" Hull shouted.

Soon, having yielded to the iron squall, the Guerrire's foremast went overboard with a crashing sound. Americans cheered like madman, sponging, priming, and firing their guns at the same time.

But the enemy had not been defeated yet – an eighteen-pound ball from the English forward gun pierced thru the Constitution's starboard gallery, then the Great Cabin, smashing a long gun and starting a fire.

And there is nothing more dangerous than fire on a wooden frigate whose decks are soaked with tar. The flames could consume a ship in minutes.

In instant the air was thick with gray smoke making breathing difficult. Blazing violently, the glowing orange was spreading fast. If it reached the ship's magazine where the powder was stored, the frigate would blow out, killing all.

"Wash-deck hoses fast! Look alive!" The commander of the stern gun division, Lt. Beckman Hoffman, shrieked organizing the battle against the fire.

Nearly blinded, with flames lapping at them, seamen rushed to execute, their hands over their faces.

Just a couple of yards away, others continued firing the guns, their eyes and lungs burning as seamen inhaled the acrid air.

Soon, water jetted into the blaze, poured from the wash-deck hose. The shovels moved rhythmically, throwing sand from the sand-tubs. Water-buckets passed from hand to hand, flew like big fat birds until the last flame went off.

The smoke hung languidly. John Brown, his eyes tearing and burning, was sponging his long gun, when an enemy bullet coming from the open port found his heart, piercing thru the sailor's back.

"No, John, no-o-o-o!" Peter Furnace ran to the dead man's side, not listening to his gun captain's commands....

At that time on the Guerriere the English captain shouted

"Boarders away! For the King!"

"For the king!" The sailors echoed.

Cheering his crew, Captain Dacres hustled up to the Guerrirere's starboard forecastle. He reached the hammocks netting at the ship's side, when a musketry ball knocked him off with a wound in his back. Having fallen on the blood stained deck, Dacres rolled over in pain.

"Captain's down! Captain's down!" The British sailors hollered in dismay.

"Get the Captain below!" The Guerriere First Lieutenant barked, leading the boarders. But he was not in luck that day either - a musket ball found him before he reached the bowsprit.

In a minute the turn of the British Second Lieutenant and then the Sailing Master came. Still the British boarders, definitely a highly-trained crew, were moving one by one over the Guerriere's bowsprit where the Yankees waited for them ready to fight. The Constitutions were so determined not to let the enemy step on their spar-deck that the English had to pull back.

In the complete darkness, the Yankee guns kept raking the enemy. A sudden thunderous crashing sound and the Guerriere's mainmast went overboard.

"Can't believe it! Looks like Yankee smashed another mast! Huzzah!" Prisoner Captain Orne cried out. The others in Guerriere's hold, joined him, shouting "Huzzah! Huzzah, Constitution!"

But the prisoners' joy faded as soon as one man murmured "Jesus, what's dat? Water is coming into de hold! We are sinking!"

The others joined him "What do we do? We'll all sink here like rats."

And just as they were mentioned, rats came from all the holes, swimming in the fast rising water and looking for shelter on the sailors' shoulders, eager to find a safer place.

Knocking the rats back down to the water, the prisoners were kicking the door "Let us out! The ship's opening a seam! Help us!"

To their despair, nobody answered. Men hurried to close the seam with the sail cloth stored in the hold, but in vain.

As the prisoners fought the flood, on the gun-deck above them John Dickenson winked to another seaman "Hey, mate, spirit room sentinel left his post. Time to get some rum, aren't you thirsty?"

The British sailor did not hesitate "Rum is the only prize we can get today. Let's go!"

Dickenson and his English mate left their dismounted gun and rushed down, followed by others. The spirit room door yielded to men's shoulders and kicks, revealing rum-barrels, all seamen's bliss. Drinking till their bellies could not take in any more, sailors dropped stone-dead right there in the spirit room hugging the barrels...

Dickenson grinned widely "Nighty night, mates! Sleep tight while I'm looking for a hammer!"

Just having pretended to drink with the others and perfectly sober, John Dickenson left the spirit room. He knew it was the time to free the prisoners. Not able to locate a hammer in that mess, Dickenson hurried up.

At that very time Captain Dacres with a dressed wound and the help of a seaman, reappeared on the weather deck to view the main, fore and mizzen masts gone. The Guerriere looked more a wreck than a ship.

"O, God!" He sighed.

"That will not do...Boarders, get back!" The English captain shouted. Then he murmured under his breath thoughtfully and bitter "There is no glory in getting people killed when there is no chance to escape."

"Sir, seamen disarmed the spirit-room sentinel, got drunk, and don't obey orders!" the Master-At-Arms reported vibrating with anger.

It was the last drop for Dacres. "I've lost the ship, and now I have lost my crew! Sure, they are not used to being defeated! But, dear God, how could all this happen?" Dacres thought, with a deep sigh. A vein was pulsing visibly at his temple.

...At that moment on the Constitution's spar-deck Hull ordered "The British is disabled! Set more sails! Haul off!"

Getting free from the Guerriere's rigging and bowsprit, the Constitution sailed off a short distance.

"Repair the rigging," ordered Hull.

The Captain feared British squadron could show up any minute. The Constitution had to be ready for a new battle.

Working non-stop, seamen set up new ropes, replaced blocks and torn out yards in the light of the battle lanterns. Always present on the spar-deck, Hull was looking attentively thru his night spy-glasses at the Guerriere, the Third Lieutenant at his side.

"Lt. Read, can not make out if she has stricken her colors. All her masts have gone. I just see a small Staff flag or Jury-mast flag on the forecastle. Hoist a boat to see whether she has struck. Ask Captain Dacres what assistance they need."

The boat was lowered in no time and started its way to the British ship that could hardly be seen in the night darkness. Just blinking stars and a rising moon lighted their way.

Soon Read, waving a white flag, climbed up the Guerriere, followed by Midshipman Henry Gilliam and seamen-rowers. Holding their lanterns high, the Yankees looked around the deck, searching for the captain.

Bosch's painting come alive opened in front of them, so surrealistic the picture was. With her masts shot away, no sails to steady her, the ship was rolling as a log in the swell. The Constitution's fire had made a slaughter-house out of the British weather deck. Sailors, ripped to pieces, blood-stained limbs, all covered with rum and molasses from the barrels that Dacres set on the deck before the battle to sweeten the victory over the Yankee he had been so sure of. Groans of the wounded sounded louder than the sea-waves. Loose guns rolled from one side to another, crushing everything on their way...

Noticing captain's gold epaulettes by their reflection under the moon light, Lt. Read headed toward Dacres.

The British Captain was standing at the rail, his shoulders dropped.

"Excuse me, Sir. Have you struck your colors?" Road asked, saluting the English Captain.

As if waking from a nightmare, Dacres said slowly "Well, all our masts are gone. I guess you might say we have struck our flag..."

In the following silence Dacres replayed the situation over and over in his mind... Then he mumbled "I wish I could keep fighting but I have...... to surrender."

"Then accept Captain Hull's compliments, Sir. He wishes to know if you need a surgeon."

"Don't you have enough business on your own ship for your surgeon?"

"Thank God, no, Sir! We have only seven wounded, and their wounds are now all dressed."

"Just seven?" Dacres asked. "How can it be?" The thought painfully hit him. Then the Captain continued "Lieutenant, we have Yankee prisoners in the hold. Go and get them, I am afraid the water is rising."

Accompanied by his crew, Lt. Read hurried downstairs. Passing thru the gun-deck they gasped seeing the mass grave where torn out arms, legs, fingers, skulls in pieces mixed with bodies of the wounded heaped, soaked in blood and splashed brains.

Even before reaching the hold, Lt. Read and his seamen heard the muffled screams. "Let us out, for God's sake!"

Then they saw John Dickenson, hammering the lock at the hold door. "C'mon! Give me a hand! They are drowning!"

With the joined efforts, the lock was smashed and the door opened. Water streamed out. Prisoners, soaked up to their waists, hugged Read and his shipmates, tears on their faces.

"God bress you, God bress you, I dought it was me last day on dis Earth!" Set free Yankees shouted as one.

"Sir, I am Captain Orne from the Yankee brig Betsey, this is my crew and this boy is Elijah Adams, a hostage from the Boston merchant the Guerriere took as a prize just yesterday. Is it true that a

Yankee frigate beat the Guerriere? True or I am dreaming?"

"Yes, the Guerriere had to surrender to the Constitution," smiled Read.

"O, Goodness, who could believe that?" said Orne, then he turned to Dickenson "Thank ye kindly, mate, for the rescue."

Dickenson, a broad-smile on his face, saluted the young Lieutenant "Sir, at ye'r command, Sir, John Dickenson, pressed from a Nantucket whaler two years back. Thankee most kindly for freeing me too! I hated to be killed for the king!"

"Welcome to freedom, John!" smiled Lieutenant Read. Then he asked all "Any wounded here? Can you keep the ship afloat until we get people from the Constitution aboard? All the British are dead, wounded or drunk."

"Aye, we will pump the water out! Mates, to the pump on the weather deck!"

Lead by the pressed sailor, prisoners rushed to the weather deck to witness the shocking picture of the battle. To his horror, Elijah Adams found himself standing in a pool of blood next to a torn-out arm. Having shut his eyes, the teenager threw up.

"Mr. Adams, get a grip! We need to pump water or this ship would sink," Captain Orne shook him.

Pumping had been going for a while on the Guerriere, when a boat came to the Constitution's starboard. Dacres was climbing up the frigate using the side ropes, Lt. Read behind him.

"Captain Dacres, give me your hand. I know you are hurt." Captain Hull stretched out his arm as if addressing an old friend.

Not expecting such gallantry from a Yankee captain, Dacres let Hull help him up on board, surprised to the core of his soul. According to Navy tradition, the English Captain saluted the Constitution quarterdeck and offered his sword to Hull.

"Captain Dacres, I will not take a sword from a man who masters it so well if you promise me not to use it while you are a prisoner."

"You have my word! It is very noble of you! Congratulations on your victory, Captain Hull. I never thought I would surrender to a Yankee," said Dacres almost fainting from loss of blood.

"How is the Guerriere? Can we tow it?"

"My beloved Guerriere is sinking, two feet of water in the hold."

"How many people aboard?"

"Two hundred sixty seven souls, sixty three wounded and fifteen dead."

"Captain Dacres, is there anything in particular that you wish to preserve?"

"Sir, if you are so kind and it is not that much trouble, I would ask for the bible that was my mother's gift. It is in my sleeping cabin."

"Lt. Read, get that bible to the captain, and start moving the wounded to the Constitution. Take surgeon Evans to help you with the wounded. The dead should go overboard; no time for a proper funeral!"

"Aye, aye, Sir! We found ten Yankee prisoners on the Guerriere, they are pumping water from the hold to keep her afloat."

"O, that's good. Mr. Read, take Mr. Carpenter and his mates and go to the Guerriere. Check if it is possible to repair her." Then, addressing a Midshipmen, "Mr. Greenlaw, place Captain Dacres into the late Lieutenant Bush's cabin!"

"This way, Sir!" Greenlaw saluted, leading the captured captain.

"The deck is yours, Lieutenant!" Hull ordered Alexander Wadsworth before leaving the quarterdeck for a little while.

♣ ♣ ♣

CHAPTER 22

AUGUST 20th 1812. OPEN SEA. FAREWELL

Hull hurried into the sick berth to check on the wounded.

Captain coming in was immediately spotted by his servant's one eye.

The full visual inspection was given to Hull's arms, legs, back, chest and head. When no wound was found, Stone sighed with a relief. Then, breaking etiquette to address an officer without given permission, he said, showing an absent tooth, "So glad, ye're well, Captain!"

The sick berth's semi-darkness could not stop the devoted servant from noticing a small detail "Don't worry about your pants. I'll fix them in no time."

Hull smiled "What would I do without you, Ivan? Get well soon," and tapped the old sailor on the shoulder. These words made the servant the happiest man on the ship.

After taking a quick look at the sick berth, the Captain was pleased to see that all wounded had already been tended by the ship's surgeon and his two mates.

"Mr. Alwyn" Hull greeted his Sailing Master who lay with an ashy face due to blood loss.

"Just a shoulder, sir!" Alwyn murmured back trying to sound firm.

"Thank you for your bravery! We won, John."

Alwyn smiled "Aye, sir!"

The Constitution's surgeon Amos Evans just moments ago had lost his battle for a seaman's life. The body still lay on what served as operating table.

"How are the wounded?" Hull asked.

Evans wiped the sweat from his forehead stained brown with old blood "Six killed and seven wounded. Two seamen -Richard Dunn and George Reynolds have nasty wounds, still there is hope for them."

"Lt. Morris is unconscious with a nasty abdominal wound, I am afraid, no hope to him." The surgeon sighed.

"I did my best. Even used spirit of wine while sewing him up." Evans pointed at the small cot.

The First Lieutenant could scarcely be recognized - he looked more dead than alive.

"He is in God's hands now." Evans said.

"Thank you, Mr. Evans. I am sure you are dead-tired but we would need your help with the Guerriere."

"Yes, Sir."

At that very moment Morris groaned and opened his eyes. After a while his sight focused and his lips mumbled something.

Lowering his head closer to the First Lieutenant's face, Hull attempted to catch the wounded man's words.

"Guns aren't firing: why? Are we all prisoners?" Morris whispered.

"My dear Charles, we are not prisoners, we are the victors! We got that bloody Guerriere! We completely mauled her!"

Despite his unbearable pain, Morris's eyes shone with joy "Now I don't fear death, my duty is fulfilled."

"Charles, fight for your life! We WILL sail together again! I'll request the Admiralty to promote you to captain's rank, you earned it with your own blood!"

"Thank you, Sir, with all my heart..."

The Captain touched Morris's hand "Have a good rest now, Charles. I am going back to my duty. The Constitution has to be repaired and be ready to fight as soon as possible".

Hull rushed up to the spar-deck to have a new foretopgallant mast set. When it was erected, the turn of the new foretopgallant yard came. Hull and Lt. Wadsworth were up all night coordinating the efforts.

At eleven in the morning Midshipman Gilliam saluted Hull "Sir, Lt. Read signals the Guerriere has five feet of water in the hold. They are pumping it out but water is gaining on them."

"Hmmm... Seems there is no way to save her. Get everyone aboard the Constitution! "

In an hour or so a boat with excited Yankee prisoners and pressed sailors from the Guerriere touched the Constitution. Although exhausted with pumping, men sang "Spanish Ladies"!

Little wonder: the joy of being free overwhelmed them. By the time of the battle they had already lost hope of seeing their land again, knowing that most likely they would be forced to die for the king....

While on the gang-ways, many kissed the Constitution's side. John Dickenson lifted his head, and was happy to see Squeaking John. Screaming "Uncle John," Dickenson hugged the old seaman.

"Hi, kiddo, you are free now!" Squeaking John smiled.

"Uncle John, where is my uncle?" asked Dickenson.
"Caleb was killed yesterday, John" murmured the old sailor. "He's with God now..."
The joy faded from Dickenson's face. "Caleb was like a father to me..."
Squeaking John nodded. "I know Caleb was a good man and a great friend too!"
The sailors nearby wanted to cheer the young man up. They joined "Caleb was a great jack tar... At least you are free now, mate!"
"Thankee kindly, for getting that Guerriere and for my freedom!" Dickenson bowed low to all.

...Later in the afternoon Lt. Read came hurriedly to the quarterdeck "Sir, all British are aboard the Constitution, but Lt. Hoffman with five men is still on the Guerriere."
"Signal to Lt. Hoffman to set Guerriere on fire! Since we can't save her, be sure she sinks."

Neither jokes nor conversations were heard on the boat heading to the Yankee frigate on its last trip from the Warrior.
The Constitution's upper deck was dead-silent, all eyes focused on the Guerriere set ablaze.
A sudden shuddering noise deafened the sailors. Bright light and fire spreading in all directions lifted the quarterdeck: the frigate broke into pieces when fire reached the powder room. Having jerked forward, the Guerriere's hull sank in no time.
Nobody said a word. Only the Purser mumbled "What a waste"...

Later that day sailors on the forecastle were sewing up the dead into their hammocks for their last trip. Marines took care of Lt. Bush and Squeaking John with John Dickenson did the same for Caleb Smith.

"Fare you well, Caleb dear! Ye saved my life thirty years ago but I let ye die yesterday!" Squeaking John said touching his friend's forehead...

"Be with God" Dickenson kissed the dead uncle before Caleb's face disappeared with the last stitch.

Next to him powder boy Peter Furnace and Seaman Hogan nearly finished sewing up John Brown. Just the upper body and the lifeless face could still be seen.

The boy's hands were shaking, he stopped, wiping tears. The blue ribbon, John Brown gave him on the boy's first night on the ship, was still tying up Peter's pony tail.

The boy, his eyes brimming with tears, made a sign to hold. After taking a simple iron cross off his neck, the only treasure in his possession that used to belong to his father, killed on the Chesapeake, the boy put it into John Brown's palm. "Ye were like a father to me" whispered Peter.

At 6 pm the new ship's bell, a trophy from the Guerriere, tolled, the old one having been shattered during the battle. The order came "Muster the crew!"

The drum rattled, calling the gathering on the upper deck.

Hull took a long look at his crew. All seamen shaved, washed, looking serious and solemn.

"Constitutions! Years from now people will remember what you fulfilled yesterday! We are the first Yankee frigate ever to beat the English!"

Dead silence. No "HUZZAH" was returned in reply. "But today we commit to the depths our shipmates, our friends, and our heroes who gave their lives for our Constitution and for our freedom:

> William Bush, First Lt. of Marines,
> Jacob Sage, seaman
> Robert Bruce, able seaman
> John Brown, able seaman
> Caleb Smith, able seaman
> James Ashford, able seaman."

Hull's voice trembled when he mouthed the name of the man who saved his life. The captain stopped, dropped his head for a moment, and then, collecting himself, started the "Gospel Of Matthew."

> "Our Father, which art in heaven,
> hallowed be thy name;
> thy kingdom come;
> thy will be done,
> on earth as it is in heaven.
> Give us this day our daily bread.
> And forgive us our trespasses,
> as we forgive them
> that trespass against us."

Foremast jacks were all ears trying to catch every word of the Lord's Prayer. A tear was slowly moving down Squeaking John's face. He didn't bother to wipe it off, deep in thought about his long-time friend, now lost forever.

> "And lead us not into temptation;

but deliver us from evil.
For thine is the kingdom,
the power, and the glory,
for ever and ever.
Amen. "

"...For eber and eber. Amen" Seaman Hogan, his
eyes closed, was repeating each word after the
captain.
"Lt. Contee, musket fire in salute to our heroes!"
ordered Hull to Lieutenant of Marines, who replaced
Lt. Bush killed in battle.
Each covered with a fifteen-star flag, the bodies
were sent to their last resting place under the sea-
water...

Later that day men gathered in the middle of the
gun deck where the auction was held - the
possessions of the deceased were put up for sale. It
was seamen's tradition to collect the money to be
enclosed into Captain's official letter to the departed
seaman's family along with his last earned wages.
Besides, why waste a dead man's belongings if
somebody else could make good use of them?
"Mates, John Brown's last thing. His pants. Twenty
cents!" The auctioneer, Ivan Stone proclaimed.
"Who's giving more?"
"Twenty cents for worn-out pants? I give fifteen!"
Asa Curtis tried his luck.
"Shame on you! Ain't ye forget, all money go to the
boy, Furnace. A widower with no children, John
Brown, would want him to have it!" The auctioneer
scolded Asa.

"Peter was like a son to him!" Old Jack joined. "I'd buy those pants myself but my butt ain't squeeze in!"

"Aye, mate, aye!" Seamen shouted from all corners.

The young seaman Hogan's heart ached – John Brown was his favorite mate. "I give fifty cents!"

Seamen gasped – nobody expected that much. But they were clearly stricken when Asa Curtis cried out "A dollar from me then!"

"A dollar for pants?" Some could not trust their ears.

"Ye're a good man, Asa!" The others supported.

"Sold!" The auctioneer hurried, not giving Asa a chance to change his mind.

While seamen boisterously discussed the last buy, Ivan Stone was making calculations. "Hat – 23 cents, shoes..." murmured he, while counting, his lips moving. Sweat dripped from the auctioneer's forehead - so intense his efforts were.

"Eleven dollars and 24 pennies!" Ivan piped at last. "The boy gets eleven dollars and 24 cents! Ha-ha! And John Brown's sea-chest!"

Proud of themselves, seamen grinned – together, they did well. Nobody dared even to dream of raising that much... It was the last thing they could do for their departed mate.

Peter Furnace though hid his face - tears were streaming down his cheeks... Even from his grave, the old John Brown was taking care of him...

"God bless you, Dear John," thought the boy. "Eleven dollars? I can not believe it! Mother can buy a goat, something she always dreamed of! Then the youngsters will have milk!" Peter recalled his brothers' hungry moans when the family did not have a morsel of food for days...

However, the auction continued. Ivan Stone lifted the right hand, his only eye sparkling with importance. "Mates, now Caleb Smith. Since he ain't got no wife nor kids, all will go to John Dickenson. John's fiancé is waiting!"

"No blessing from her father 'til Dickenson has a small boat," added Squeaking John.

"Ain't be greedy, mates! Caleb's looking at you right now!" Old Jack shouted.

"Here's the mermaid, Caleb curved from walrus's tusk!" started Ivan Stone.

"Seventy five cents!" Hogan felt very generous and in fact three quarters of a dollar was one third of what his tiny sock, which served as a purse, held.

"More?" asked Stone. After making sure that nobody was willing to give a better price, he said "This is a special item. Captain wanted to buy it, if no one else ain't pay more. Let's see how much Captain is willing to pay..."

Ivan Stone produced a small purse and drew out a pack of banknotes. His audience stopped breathing while he was counting.

"Fifty dollars! Fifty dollars? Ye, fifty dollars! Wow! Who's giving more?"

At the sound of these words, John Dickenson's heart leapt. All men present were astonished to the core of their souls too - the price was way too high.

"Fifty dollars?" Hogan shook his head, refusing to believe it. "I ain't saw that much in my life!"

"Captain says Caleb taught him when he was just nine. That's probably why." Stone said. "He wanted to help John too."

All eyes turned to look at the fortunate man.

John, his face beaming, doubled over, bowing low. "Thank you, mates! The Constitution brought me good luck."

"Now I got the money for a boat... Enough to fix the old house too. If Marie could wait for me..." John was thinking.

...With all sails set to make the fastest way home, the overcrowded Constitution with two hundred sixty seven English prisoners aboard glided to Boston. To keep the crew ready to fight, Hull beat to quarters four times on his way to the port.

All seamen worked days and nights reefing and setting sails, no complaints heard - they knew the British frigates roamed somewhere near.

Finally, the familiar Boston Lighthouse cut thru the foggy night, lifting up their spirits. Two more days and they would be safely in Boston's harbor. It was only then that Captain Hull found a moment to write an official letter to the Admiralty.

"US Frigate Constitution
Off Boston Light
August 28th 1812

Sir,
I have an Honor to inform you that on the 19th inst. at 2 pm being in Latitude 41' 42" Longitude 55' 48" with the Constitution under my command..."

After making a short dry description of the victory, Hull turned to his crew's efforts. There his words flew freely.

"You can have no doubt of the gallantry, and good conduct of the officers and ship's company I have the honor to command. All fought with great bravery; and it gives me great pleasure to say that from the smallest boy in the ship to the oldest seamen, not a look of fear was seen."

As Hull wrote "not a look of fear was seen" the battle scenes arose in his mind: James Ashford protecting him with his own body, Caleb Smith dying with a splinter in his chest, Lt. Bush dropping dead...

Just yards from the Great Cabin, a deck below, in the small cabin that used to belong to late Lieutenant of Marines, the wounded British Captain leaned over the tiny desk, writing a report to his superior. With words getting stuck in his mind, Dacres had to force himself to get them on paper: "...The Guerriere was so cut up, that all attempts to get her in would have been useless. As soon as the wounded were got out of her, they set her on fire, and I feel in my duty to state the conduct of Captain Hull and his Officers to our Men has been that of a brave Enemy, the greatest care being taken to prevent our Men loosing the smallest trifle, and the greatest attention being paid to the wounded."

♣ ♣ ♣

CHAPTER 23

AUGUST 29th 1812. OPEN SEA.
BACK TO BOSTON

Fifteen excited midshipmen sat under a single dimly lit lamp. The flame flickered in their eyes.
"Lads, hard to believe, but the battle took just half an hour!" Midshipman Salter said.
"Aye, indeed!" The others laughed merrily.
Midshipman Henry Gilliam, the oldest among them, did not smile. At twenty two, he had already started to value human life: "You know, lads, you should see their deck. It was like a nightmare: skulls in pieces, legs, arms and blood...in every direction. The loose guns rolled in the swell crushing everything. ...It is staying in my eyes..."
"God!" Midshipman German started throwing up.
"Common, mate, you are alive!" Young Greenlaw said.
"Guess they were sure they would win." Salter added.
"They sure were! A British frigate never surrendered to a Yankee."
The last word reminded midshipman Greenlaw of the Yankee-Doodle song. He piped it aloud:

"Yankee Doodle went to town
A-riding on a pony,
Stuck a feather in his cap
And called it macaroni."

Greenlaw winked to the others who joined eagerly:

> "Yankee Doodle keep it up,
> Yankee Doodle dandy,
> Mind the music and the step,
> And with the girls be handy"

The boys felt happy just to be alive. They were too young to die and too young for the horrors of the war...

Next morning at dawn Lieutenant Shubrick was given an order to go ashore with dispatches bound for Washington.

"God Speed, John!" Hull waved his hand when the Lieutenant dropped into the cutter.

"Aye, Aye, Sir!" saluted Shubrick, not able to suppress a wide-smile. A stroke of luck: he was to deliver happy news to the Admiralty.

Meanwhile, the Constitution sailed proudly on the tide to Boston, fifteen stars and fifteen stripes flags flowing from the tops of all her masts. A long pennant on the main mast - fifteen vertical white, red, and white stripes close to the mast with a blue swallow tail, hovered and coiled as a large snake up in the sky.

Colored signal flags made by seamen, as bright as the rainbow, decorated the frigate's rigging when it glided near Boston's Lighthouse.

A small ancient boat came alongside. "Constitution, ahoy! What news?" A scrawny, weather-beaten fisherman shouted.

"Victory over Guerriere!" Midshipman German cried back.

"Nah, kidding there?"

"No kidding, chap! The Guerriere is burnt up!"

"That ain't possible!" A minute passed before the fisherman collected himself to mumble in response.

Sailors on Constitution forecastle burst out laughing.

"That IS true, mate! We burned it!"

"That ghost frigate with large letters 'Guerriere' on its sail?"

"Aye, the same one!"

"Too good to be true! Yankee beating an English ship?" the fisherman stood like a statue in his small boat, then realizing that the sailors were not joking, made up his mind.

"Then the fishing is done, I'll go to Boston and let everybody know the news!"

Another burst of laughter shook the Constitution spar-deck.

The old fisherman could not wait for the tide. He sped right to the shore.

There, a young man who was loading a barrel into his small boat suddenly heard "Hey, Billy! Take my horse and ride to Boston! Ye will be there before the tide turns in!"

"What's the rush? And why ye're so kind today to give me ye'r horse? Ye ain't sick, are ye?"

"Great news! The Constitution defeated the Guerriere! And burnt it!"

Billy dropped the barrel "Drunk too much, lad? It can not be!"

"It is what the Constitutions told I!"

"What am I standing here for then? God, what news!"

Having forgotten about his chores, Billy ran to get a horse. After jumping into the saddle and God-knows-how managing to hold a fifteen-star flag and the rein, he galloped to Boston leaving behind clouds of dust.

In the neighboring village, hens dug the dirt in a quiet, sleepy street not giving attention to the two men discussing sad war news. At the sound of hooves, the villagers turned their heads "Is that fellow crazy or something? Oh, look, he is waving a flag!"

Billy's horse slowed down.

"Hurrying to Hell, guy?" an older man asked.

Billy was not offended "Great news! The Constitution defeated the Guerriere! On the morning tide the Constitution will be in Boston!" and with a broad smile rode off.

It took a while for the villagers to comprehend such news.

"Oh, God, defeated the Guerriere? No joke? C'mon, Bob, let's go to Boston!"

"Let's tell the news to the neighbors first and I am on my way!"

Both men ran around with shouts "The Constitution defeated bloody Guerriere!"

The news spread like fire. Women with toddlers in their arms, children, their fathers, and the elderly filled the street hollering, laughing and crying with happiness... Just days before the news of Fort Dearborn (modern Chicago) massacred by Indians provoked by the British was received. Then another story came about American Forces surrendering

Detroit. To make things worse, rumors spread about the frigate Guerriere robbing the shore towns nearby.

Fear kept the Massachusetts folks up all night... "No hope left" everyone thought... And suddenly such a victory!

Overwhelmed by joy, villagers saddled the horses, filled in carts and headed to Boston.

Indeed, Billy the fisherman was a fast news-deliverer: all small boats waved flags and handkerchiefs when the Constitution was slowly making her way to the harbor.

"Constitution, ahoy! The Guerrirere is beaten!"

"Viva the Constitution!"

"Huzzah, the Constitution!"

Boston harbor wharf at last. The flotilla of small boats, all in flying flags and banners, greeted the heroic frigate –nobody went fishing that day!

Even fishermen from Cape Cod, Marta's Vineyard and Nantucket all came. Nobody remembered such a merry gathering of the kind. A huge crowd was expecting the Constitution ashore. Men holding flags high, women waving hats and handkerchiefs, children with wild flowers...

Fifteen star flags decorated every building. Not a single window was without people leaning out eager to meet their dear ship.

The Boston battery saluted the Constitution, hailing the brave frigate. The roar of its guns filled the harbor and echoed far away.

The Constitution's cannons replied with thundering booms. The sound of the last shot had not died out yet as tremendous roar "Huzzah, Constitution" made the air tremble....

Seamen on the forecastle savored the moment speechless.

"I ain't saw nothing like that in all my bloody life," finally mumbled the captain's servant Ivan Stone, his only good eye watering. A stained bandage still covered the other. Stone jabbed an elbow in Squeaking John's side.

"They welcome us like heroes." John added proudly, pointing his bent finger at the crowd. Tears sparkled on the old sailor's cheeks "I wish my chap, Caleb Smith could see it!"

Twisting his head around, ex-pressed and now freed sailor, John Dickenson, was looking for his dear Marie in the crowd. What if his beautiful fiancé was there, waiting?

Orders to drop an anchor followed: "All hands, bring ship to anchor! Stand by to take in the flying jib, royals, and studdingsails! Haul taut! Shorten sail! Helm a-lee! Stand clear of the starboard cable! Stream the buoy! Let go the anchor! Man the sparker brails! Brail up the spanker!"

The commands were hardly heard, being covered by loud cheers from the crowd. Knowing their trade well, seamen on the masts coordinated their efforts themselves: no orders could reach them in that noise. Proud, confused and flattered they were receiving so much attention...

It was a matter of some hours when Lt. Read reported "Sir, all wounded are moved to the Boston hospital."

"Good, start landing the prisoners!" ordered Hull.

"Sir, Commodore Bainbridge to see you." Midshipman Gilliam appeared, running out of breath to the quarter-deck.

"Pipe the Commodore aboard!"

The boatswain Adams sprang a ceremonial call, when Bainbridge stepped on the starboard gangway saluting the quarterdeck according to Navy tradition.

"Congratulations, Hull, what a victory! Who could think it was possible?" the Commodore shook Hull's hand.

"But how dare you sail without orders? Do you know what you'd deserved should the British have captured you? By the court-martial you would be hanged from the yardarm!"

"Commodore Bainbridge, I am perfectly aware of that and did so to show the Admiralty what the US Navy is capable of. As for the Constitution, I am the one to know best her excellent sailing qualities and with such a crew any ship can be outsailed." Hull replied coldly.

"What about the British gunnery? No Yankee could match it even close."

"Commodore Bainbridge, you are not quite right. The Constitution's guns bore faster and more accurate than those of the Guerriere's "

"Anyway, I have orders to take over the Constitution. In fact, I had the order the day you sailed off. You are to take the Constellation."

The news shocked everyone on the deck including Hull. Lt Read, the officer-of the-watch, murmured "Bloody hell!"

But Bainbridge had not finished yet "By the way, I am sorry to say your brother William died when you were on your cruise. You are to take care of his widow and children."

That blow crucified the brave captain. Having collected himself, he said "Commodore Bainbridge, I will fix my brother's business fast. But I must insist on the Constitution. We have the war at hand."

"The Constitution is mine! This is an order!" barked Bainbridge. Then realizing that with such a victory the Admiralty might not refuse Hull's request, he said "Give me a chance to distinguish myself too!"

♣ ♣ ♣

CHAPTER 24

AUGUST 30 1812. Boston. ARE YOU A GHOST?

Once the wounded sailors from both frigates were moved to the hospital, the turn came for the Yankee prisoners and pressed sailors freed from the Guerriere.

Before leaving the Constitution's deck, some seamen bowed low, almost touching the spar-deck floor, others kissed the frigate's sides and its carronades – they knew, if not for this ship, they would never have seen their country again.

The teenager Elijah Adams hurried straight to his home, eager to see his parents and tell the news about his unexpected liberation.

Sudbury Street was quiet – all the inhabitants left for the harbor to see the legendary ship. When Elijah knocked on the old dark oak door, he had to wait quite long until the sound of his mother's rheumatic feet, shuffling on the stone floor, reached his ears.

"Who's there?"

"Mom, it's me, Elijah!"

Hardly audible exclamation and the door shot open.

"My son!" The old woman hugged Elijah and stood like that for a long while, scared to let him out of her grip.

"But where is your father? Did the brig sink? All, but you?"

Having entered the house the boy smiled "Don't worry, mother, dad is alive!"

Soon Elijah sat at the small kitchen table. His mother, her face glowing with happiness, was fussing around setting all of the provisions she had for her dear child. Ham, dark pumpernickel bread, butter, a jug of butter-milk were added to a plate with cut tomatoes, onions and green apples.

The boy could hardly wait for his mother to take a seat to say a prayer. Puritan customs were strictly followed in the house.

When his mother turned her back to the boy, he quickly shoveled a piece of an apple into his mouth and chewed it, enjoying the forgotten taste. Sour apple juice seemed like heaven after all that salted pork, dry pies and ship biscuits every day.

"Elijah, tell me what happened and where your father is?" the woman asked when she thought her son's hunger was satisfied.

The boy wiped off his lips with his left hand but could not help it and took another drought of butter-milk before starting his story.

"We left the coast of Portugal a month ago with cargo of silk and salt. The brig was not far from our North Atlantic shores when a British frigate appeared. Father gave the order to set all sails to flee. But our small ship heavily loaded was too slow. In an hour the British were aboard. They robbed us of all our silk. They would have taken the ship as well but the British had captured so many ships as prizes, there were no spare hands left to sail our brig to their blockading station in Nova Scotia. They took me aboard as a hostage instead to make father bring them a five thousand dollar note payable to their agent in Boston."

Nicholas Orloff

The boy's mother lifted her arms in despair "They took our silk and wanted five thousand dollars more? My God, where will my husband get it? He borrowed the money before sailing off to Portugal to buy silk…"

The boy nodded sadly and continued "Thus I became a prisoner on His Majesty's Ship 'Guerriere' among another ten men from Yankee merchants, tightly packed into the hold. I can't even tell you what we ate and drank."

The teenager took a slice of apple, chewed it slowly, and then continued.

"At least, I had hope to be set free if father sent the money. The others knew they would be forced into the king's Navy and most likely never see their families again."

Tears sparkled on the old woman's wrinkled face. "God, then how you are here?"

"O, mother, God saved me! On August 19th our brave Constitution met us in the Atlantic. All prisoners including old Captain Orne were scared that the Guerriere will take her as a prize. We prayed for her! A hundred "Our Father", no less, I sent to God." The boy said smiling.

"Our frigate went into battle and won! Dear mother, you should have heard the thunder of our cannons and long guns! You should have felt how the British frigate shook when its mizzen mast was shot away! The Guerriere's seam opened and we would have drowned in the hold if the Constitution sailors had not freed us!"

Elijah's mother crossed herself with a shaken hand.

"Mother, our frigate – they are heroes! Real heroes" The boy exclaimed waiving his hands in the air.

"And thus today the Constitution reached the Boston harbor making me free and safe with you!" Elijah hugged his mother. "Father should come soon too. I thought he would be in by now."

The boy was right - in the middle of the next night a loud knock at the front door woke him up. Starting a candle-end, Elijah hurried down hoping to see his father.

When the boy opened the door, his dad began crossing himself, frozen by an unexpected meeting "Dear God, bless me!"

The old sailor rubbed his eyes "Are you a ghost?"

"Father, it's me, Elijah!" laughed the teenager. "Don't be afraid, you can touch me!"

"Where the hell did you come from?" The man still could not believe his own eyes. Then feeling the warmth of his son's body, the old skipper broke down sobbing.

It was the first time Elijah saw his dad, the old salt, crying.

The teenager hugged his father "The Constitution freed us soon after you sailed off. I got here yesterday!"

...As for John Dickenson, it was only the next day when a small fishing boat took him to Nantucket. John's heart was beating hard: did Marie wait for him?

"Almost three years passed, she might have been forced to get married. Her father said - two years... "

John didn't know that a day before Marie's father agreed to wait just a week before giving his daughter's hand to a widower with three children.

"No news from John for three years. He is probably lying somewhere on the sea-bottom. Your life is passing by... It's against God's will for a woman to be alone. Besides, if I die tomorrow, who will take care of you?" The old man asked Marie, then trying to comfort her "The widower ain't a bad man. He's got a small boat. At least you won't be hungry!"

Marie sobbed "Father, give me a week, maybe the Constitution has some news about John." The rumors about the battle had just reached the island.

"A week, not more" were her father's words and no woman in a Puritan family could disobey.

"The matchmaker said the widower had another girl in mind. All I can do is to ask for a week delay."

...Having reached the island's rocky shore, John Dickenson ran fast as the wind all the way to Marie's tiny house, taking well-remembered shortcuts. John's heart pounded, blood whooshed through his ears. The next slope up and a small field opened in front of him.

Were his eyes playing tricks – his Marie was digging out potatoes, all alone. Hard work for a woman, her black cap awry, red hair curled in the wind shining gold in tender afternoon light. Her dark blouse with rolled up sleeves showed the sun-tanned slender arms. A country girl, still her movements were gracious even when she was thrusting the shovel deep into the soil.

Busy at work, Marie did not see her fiancé coming. Still not believing his eyes, John stopped motionless taking in the picture. For so many days he had been dreaming about this minute and now his legs failed him - he simply could not make them move.

As if feeling something, Marie turned her head...
The girl's eyes opened wide, the shovel fell into a
potato bush. With arms spinning Marie ran toward
her fiancé "Jo-o–o-h-n."

The sound of her voice made the man speed forward
as fast as if he were flying. Taking Marie in his
arms, John whirled the girl in the air, holding her
tight.

They were just two more lives saved by the
Constitution...

♣ ♣ ♣

CHAPTER 25

NOVEMBER 1812. WASHINGTON.
NEXT TO IMPOSSIBLE

A month passed and a stone was erected on Isaac Hull's younger brother's grave. All creditors were paid off. The rest of Captain Hull's money went to his mourning sister-in-law. Thirty years old, two children and already a widow... Her beauty faded within a month. At least, the house that the creditors had threatened to take away was saved. The money the older brother had provided would help the family stay afloat for some time.

"When I get a ship, I will keep sending money to support this family," thought Hull, "Why do I need money? No wife, no children. I don't need much."

Never in his life had Hull felt so lonely. Every person he met congratulated him on his victory. The hand-written bulletins spread out, reaching the West. Salutes sounded in the celebration of the Constitution's victory. It was supposed to feel good, why then was he so run down? In the middle of a war and a captain without a ship, how could he be happy? The Constellation was somewhere in the Atlantic. His Constitution under the command of Commodore Bainbridge had also sailed off. The crew tried to get their Captain back but those that openly said a word against Bainbridge were sent to gun-boats.

"No frigates left. I will take anything that can float
– a sloop, a brig, anything, just to sail towards the
enemy." With these thoughts Hull headed to
Washington hoping to get an audience with the
Secretary of the Admiralty.

At last, the long awaited day came when Hull
slowly took the Admiralty steps, collecting the words
he would say to Secretary Hamilton, begging him to
give him any ship.

Contrary to tradition, the captain did not have to
wait a single minute past the time set for the
appointment. As soon as he placed himself
comfortably into a corner chair ready to linger to be
called, the Admiralty aide bowed saying "Captain
Hull, His Honor Secretary Hamilton will see you
now!"

Surprised, Isaac crossed the waiting room and
stepped into the secretary's parlor. Secretary Paul
Hamilton, a wide-smile on his face, stood up from
the chair at the table and greeted Hull at the door.

"Dear Captain Hull! Congratulations, what a
victory! And just a few casualties! Who could think a
Yankee frigate could do it? George Washington was
right about building our Navy!"

Hamilton shook hands with Hull, and even hugged
him, which was completely unusual: all the
Captains, even Commodores addressed Hamilton as
"your obedient humble servant".

"I am proud of you, Hull!"

"Sir, I must mention that it was possible only due
to the bravery of the crew and the officers. In spite of
the heavy enemy fire, Lieutenant of Marines Bush,
First Lieutenant Morris and the sailing Master
Alwyn led the boarders. Lieutenant Bush was killed,

Morris and Alwyn wounded. I think both deserve promotion!"

"Dear Hull, I have good news! The Secretary has already approved your request. Lieutenant Morris is promoted to Captain and the Sailing Master Alwyn to Lieutenant!"

Hull bowed "Very much obliged, Sir!"

"But that is not all. I just received the news from Congress. A gold medal to you and silver medals to all your officers along with fifty thousand dollars of prize were voted for the crew!"

"Thank you, Sir! I am honored!" said Hull, hand at his heart. Then he continued "However, please don't consider me unthankful. I am begging the Secretary to give me a ship for another cruise."

"Hm... All eight frigates have their captains already. But wait... The Secretary will not refuse our War Hero. We will proceed with the replacement if you wish."

Hamilton took a seat at the table and pointed at a chair.

"Captain, the Secretary has an important assignment for you. In fact, I think that you are the only one who is up to the task." Hamilton studied Hull's expression.

"Sir?"

"After your glorious victory the Congress decided to build the first US Navy ship-of-the line that will carry 74-guns! However, the sum they have saved is not enough to build even a smaller ship. You know, the only available ship yard is in Portsmouth, New Hampshire with just a handful of small buildings and no wharf at all, to complicate the task. Only eighteen men in the whole yard, not a single guard nor cannon! More than that, three hundred miles of coastline around it are defenseless. The British feel pretty much at home there! They rob the shore villages! "

Hamilton stopped and looked at Hull then continued. "You are to build the defense line, the ship yard and ship-of-the-line 'Washington'! Just that... Next to impossible. Anyway, defeating the Guerriere was no easy task, but you succeeded. The Secretary has chosen you to accomplish this.

"Sir, anything in my power for my country!"

"Thank you, Hull! I knew the Admiralty could count on you!" Hamilton said smiling.

♣ ♣ ♣

CHAPTER 26

NOVEMBER 1812. NEW YORK.
COULD IT BE TRUE?

...For years New Yorkers kept talking about the banquet given to Captain I. Hull.

The city hall, decorated with Yankee flags, was filled with well-dressed gentlemen and beautiful ladies. Precious stones in diadems and necklaces sparkled, catching candle lights. Ladies' silk evening gowns brought from London or even from Paris rustled. Rose oil scent filled the air.

To make the marvel complete, each colonnade looked like a frigate mast and a miniature ship was set on every table.

The guest-of-honor, Captain Hull, gold epaulette on his shoulders, was seated at the front table.

New York City Mayor DeWitt Clinton started his speech at the podium.

"Ladies and gentlemen! We are gathered here today to celebrate the victory that even two hundred years from now people will be talking about!"

The audience burst with applause. DeWitt waited for silence to drop and continued.

"Remember what the British Chronicle used to say about the US small fleet, and about the frigate Constitution? "A bundle of pine boards". Would you like to hear what they say now?" Clinton asked, smiling and getting the issue of "The British Naval Chronicle" closer to his eyes.

"It reads 'had the Guerriere's men been half as well skilled in the use of great guns as Constitution were, the proportion of killed and wounded would not have been so great nor one ship made a complete wreck of while the other suffered no material injury in hull or rigging' ".

DeWitt Clinton removed the paper and looked proudly at the public.

"No one thought it would be possible to defeat the Guerriere – one of the best British frigates under the great Captain Dacres. Just a great leader with the perfect seamanship could perform that!"

A storm of shouts "Bravo", "Huzzah to Captain Hull" shook the building. The mayor clapped his hands with the others.

"The government thought our frigates should not sail further than the tide because of the powerful British Navy. Captain Hull proved that even a handful of frigates can provide security of our shore and merchant trades!"

New squall of applause and shouts "Bravo to the brave hero!" filled the air.

"Ladies and Gentlemen, behold the great citizen of our country, Captain Isaac Hull!"

A standing ovation made the City Hall look like a stormy sea. Flattered, Hull stood up and bowed, his right hand on his heart.

"Ladies and Gentlemen, it is my honor today to say that we, thankful citizens of New York, present Captain Hull a freedom of the city and a sword!" announced DeWitt.

Squalls of "huzzah" overflew the city hall when Hull stepped to the podium to receive the sword.

Having kissed its blade, the captain held it high.
"For our country! For our nation!"
A roar of cheers erupted, reminding the captain of the moment in the battle with the Guerriere when its mizzen went overboard.
After all his vigorous claps the mayor's hands hurt. Clearing his throat, DeWitt said loudly "And now our famous poet Philip Freneau presents his new song "On the capture of the Guerriere".
A 60-year old man came up to the podium. As ever, his muse hasn't failed this time. In 1778 the poet sailed on a Yankee privateer and was captured. He spent six weeks in the hell of the prison ship "Jersey" and was about to die. Having been exchanged, he survived, treasuring freedom more than anything else for the rest of his life. Nothing could inspire him better than the Constitution's victory.

"Long the Tyrant of our coast
Reign'd the famous Guerriere;
Our little navy she defy'd.
Public ship and privateer:
On her sails in letters red,
To our captains were display'd
Words of warning, words of dread,
All, who meet me, have a care!
I am England's Guerriere!

On the wide, Atlantic deep
(Not her equal for the fight)
The Constitution, on her way,
Chanced to meet these men of might:
On her sails was nothing said,

But her waist the teeth displayed
That a deal of blood could shed,
Which, if she would venture near,
Would stain the decks of the Guerriere.

Now our gallant ship they met
And, to struggle with John Bull
Who had come, they little thought,
Strangers, yet, to Isaac Hull:
Better, soon, to be acquainted:
Isaac hail's the lord's anointed
While the crew the cannon pointed,
And the balls were so directed
With a blaze so unexpected;

Isaac did so maul and rake her
That the decks of Captain Dacres
Were in such a woeful pickle
As if death, with scythe and sickle,
With his sling, or with his shaft
Had cut his harvest fore and aft.
Thus, in thirty minutes ended,
Mischiefs that could not be mended:
Masts, and yards, and ship descended,
All to Davy Jones' locker
Such a ship in such a pucker!

Drink about to the Constitution!
She perform'd some execution
Did some share of retribution
For the insults of the year
When she took the Guerriere."

Laughter, merry exclamations, applause and even tears roused by the poem, were a great reward for the old poet.

But everything comes to an end, even celebrations. The wine was drunk, the dishes emptied, and gentlemen shook Hull's hands expressing respect and admiration.

"Congratulations, Captain! What a victory! It will belong to history of our country!" a man was saying.

One gentleman, while waiting for his turn, stared at the ladies. "What a strange necklace that marvelous lady is wearing! What's that?"

Hull turned his head, meeting bright, sparkling eyes of a young lady in her early twenties. The beauty of her slim figure, her gracious, confident movements struck him motionless.

Somehow her face looked familiar. Where could he have seen those dark-brown eyes with hazelnut speckles glowing gold in candle lights?

Hull's sight was caught by an unusual necklace too. Suddenly he recognized a piece of rope he gave to a young girl visiting the Constitution ten years back...

Could it be true? A thin teenage girl with hazel eyes full of dreams of the sea and this astonishing beauty? Dear Ann Hart...

For a long while Hull and Ann were looking at each other. The hall disappeared, all conversations faded away - there were just the two of them in the whole world.

As if waking up, Hull bowed to a gentleman waiting for him. "May I be excused?"

The captain, amazement in his eyes, walked to Ann, still not able to believe it was her, the young girl from his lonely dreams.

"Miss Ann McCurdy Hart from Connecticut, is it really you?"

Ann felt blood rushing to her face. She had never stopped thinking about the handsome lieutenant and wished to meet him again. Every evening, while alone, she would open a box containing old newspapers with articles about the Constitution and her captain...

Trying to compose herself with tears brimming in her eyes she whispered "You still remember my name?"

"How could I forget? All these years you were like a lighthouse for me. You always lead me ashore."

Ann's eyes shone and a smile brightened her face. Hull repeated the words she pronounced the day they met.

"I could not forget either. All these ten years I prayed to God to help you and the Constitution."

Hull bowed and kissed Ann's hand not able to keep his eyes away from hers.

"But God, those deep eyes that warmed my heart for so many years. Isn't it a dream?" He could not stop asking himself...

People say one should wait for a soul-mate. Some find their true love in their youth. Others spend years in search...

...Not a month passed before the sounds of the old pipe organ filled the old Say Brook church.

Wearing a white lace dress under a long white veil, dazzling Ann Marie Hart slowly walked along the church aisle proudly lead by her father, Captain Elisha Hart.

All guests, her mother Jeannette McCurdy of Lyme, her four sisters, close friends and relatives followed the movements of the bride, known as the most beautiful and intelligent woman of Connecticut. Ann's father, a successful merchant whose store and mansion still can be seen on Main Street in Say Brook, provided the best education for his daughters Sarah, Ann, Elizabeth, Amelia and Jeannette. The wonder of the neighborhood - a piano was shipped from London, the first in Say Brook. Literature, music, history, art, foreign languages were in the possession of Elisha's Hart daughters... The best grooms from Connecticut, Massachusetts, and New York sought Ann's hand. But none of them seemed to be able to reach Ann's heart.

In front of the altar Hull was waiting for Ann. His gold captain's epaulettes glistened by the light of the curious sun sending its rays thru the colored-glass window.
"Is it true and I would never be alone again?"
Lifting Ann's veil, the war hero met her eyes sparkling with excitement.
"Since my childhood I was sure there was nothing in the world more beautiful than the sea. But I was wrong..." The thought came to Hull's mind.
He whispered "I love you", Ann mouthed back without sound, so that only Hull could catch: "Love you back, my dear captain" and smiled.
As from far away the minister's words sounded.
"Dear beloved, we are gathered here in the sight of God, and in the face of this congregation, to join together this man and this woman in Holy Matrimony. Today, in the middle of War we

celebrate love that our God sent us as a high hope that mankind will get thru all the pain, blood and death and a new life will start." A philosopher and a poet sounded in the minister's words...

"Do you, Captain Hull, take this woman to be your lawfully wedded wife, to have and to hold, to love and cherish her as long as you both shall live?"

"Yes, I do, with all my heart." Love and happiness glowed in Hull's eyes, taking away years of hard life and loneliness.

"Do you, Ann Hart, take this man to be your lawfully wedded husband, to love and to cherish?"

At these words, the brave captain's heart began hammering louder than in a battle. What if she said 'no'? He still could not believe that his love at first sight came true. The love, cherished as a dream, without any hope.

But Ann, blood in her face, answered almost too quickly "Yes, Yes, I do, with all my soul!"

Hull exhaled with relief and smiled repeating after the priest:

> "With this ring, I thee wed.
> With my body, I thee honor.
> And all my worldly goods with
> thee I share. In the name of the
> Father and of the Son, and of the
> Holy Ghost. Amen."

...Two months passed since their quiet wedding as the Constitution's white sails brought the news about another great Yankee victory: the British frigate "Java" was defeated! According to

Commodore Bainbridge "He never knew such a trained and spirited crew as the Constitution's."

Proud, Isaac Hull met the frigate at the Boston wharf and paraded her officers up State Street to Faneuil Hall where a great dinner was given in honor of the Constitution!

However, Hull's heart was aching – many officers and seamen, his dear mates, who shared tough times with him, were killed in battle. His young sailing master John Alwyn, promoted to Lieutenant, was one of them.

Hull hid his tears when he was told about the fatally-wounded seaman James Cheever. James, lying in the pool of his blood next to the dead Squeaking John, at a cry "Enemy struck her colors!" lifted himself on one elbow, and gave three cheers before dropping dead...

♣ ♣ ♣

CHAPTER 27

JULY 1840. MEDITERRANIAN.
FOR A LONG, LONG TIME

Twenty eight years passed... No doubt, the holy union that joined Hull and his wife Ann was created above in the sky. Nothing could shake their love and care for each other, even the War. Always at her husband's side, Ann went to sea with him. It was unheard of – a woman on a warship!

Perfectly aware of danger, she risked her life while Hull was building Portsmouth Naval Shipyard, surrounded by the enemy. All day long alone in the cold old Portsmouth house, she was waiting for her husband to come home from the shipyard on Fernald's Island.

Rumors flew about the English frigates lurking nearby eager to burn the yard and put the new ship soon ready for sea on fire....

How could the young woman, grown up in the luxury of her father's house and belonging to the most brilliant society, find the strength to endure those difficulties? No doubt their love gave her wings...

Ann shared all the victories with her husband. She was proud and happy for him when on the first of October of 1814 in the middle of war Captain Hull launched the 74-gun ship-of-the-line "Washington" - the first two-decker in the American Navy! Her dear captain had accomplished the impossible again...

Today, two hundred years later, the Portsmouth Naval Shipyard that Isaac Hull built is the main Naval Shipyard for nuclear-powered ships and submarines.

Hull kept his word – his First Lieutenant Charles Morris was promoted to captain. Later Morris hoisted the commodore's broad pendant. It was a miracle - Morris survived his wound. Squeaking John's luck was passed to him... Just years later medical science would realize the power of the spirit of wine on the battle wounds...

...Twenty eight years passed and silver plates with crystal glasses sparkled on a beautifully-decorated table with a fine table-cloth in the middle of the Great Cabin of His Majesty's flag ship "Vernon".

The epicurean dishes produced by the Admiral's private French chef, colored the table with pink lobsters, brown ducks stuffed with truffles and creamy oyster bisque. Green and yellow grapes completed the splendid picture.

The gold epaulets shone on shoulders of the British Mediterranean squadron ship's captains. The soft breeze, filled with the aroma of Italian olives, coming from the open stern windows, fanned the Great Cabin, making everybody comfortable.

The loud and merry conversation stopped when the British rear-admiral James Dacres roused, a glass of wine reflected dark crimson in his hand.

"Dear guests with this twelve-year old precious Madeira I would like to suggest a toast to my closest friend, the commander of the US Mediterranean squadron Admiral Isaac Hull. Our friendship had an unusual start. It began on the day Captain's Hull

Constitution defeated me and my beloved Guerriere."

The smiles faded away on the faces of the British officers.

"We, in the British Navy, laughed at the Constitution and called her "bundle of pine boards sailing under a bit of striped bunting". When it came to fighting, it was another thing. It took only 30 minutes for that bundle of pine boards to completely maul the Guerriere, the crack ship! It was a shock for me and all His Majesty's Navy. But the bigger surprise was the gallant way the Yankee treated us, the prisoners of war. Captain Hull made sure that even a morsel of my crew's belongings would be saved."

Dacres made a sign to his servant standing behind his chair to pass the large book. "This is my very treasure - the bible my mother gave me. Captain Hull saved it from the sinking Guerriere and let me have it. For the outstanding captain and a gentleman, Admiral Hull!"

"For Admiral Hull!" All British officers hailed rising.

Isaac Hull, still energetic in his late sixties despite his grown belly, thanked the host, flattered. His wife Ann, still beautiful after almost thirty years of marriage, smiled quietly.

"Mrs. Hull, it must be tough on you to stay on a warship?" Admiral Dacres asked.

"Oh, no, not at all! Being a sailor was my childhood dream. Besides, I can not stand to be parted from my dear husband." Ann exclaimed without any trace of hesitation.

A happy impression touched Hull's face "I know, it is against the rules to have admiral's wife on the flag ship: it doesn't help to discipline the crew. The truth is I was waiting for so long that I just simply could not get separated from Ann anymore!"

Hull's eyes met his wife's making the old admiral aware of her full understanding and endless love.

"Let this marriage be blessed!" Dacres raised his glass.

"Admiral, where is the Constitution now? Is she still in the service? Is it true that she has never been defeated? The British admiral asked.

"Yes, she is in the service. Right now she is the flag ship of the Pacific squadron," the Yankee Admiral did not even try to hide his pride.

"Unbelievable, she was launched in 1797, was she not? Forty three years old! She beats all the odds then! On average, a ship's life is fifteen years, not more. But surely the Constitution can not be such a great sailing ship as she used to be!"

"On the contrary, when in 1830 The Navy Admiralty decided to break the Constitution down, the whole country stood up. Poet Oliver Wendell Holmes wrote a poem "Old Ironsides". Let me recall..." Hull took a moment then recited the poem

"Her deck, once red with heroes' blood,
Where knelt the vanquished foe,
When winds were hurrying o'er the flood
And waves were white below,
No more shall feel the victor's tread,
Or know the conquered knee;--
The harpies of the shore shall pluck
The eagle of the sea! "

Smiling, Hull continued "All the country collected money for the Constitution's repair. She was dry-docked and re-built. She IS a great sailor that was NEVER defeated!"

The English Admiral rose up. "My distinguished guests! His Majesty's officers! Please raise your glasses for the outstanding ship, frigate Constitution! Let her never be defeated and let her proudly sail for long, long years!"

Having lifted their glasses and standing up, all guests repeated Dacres's last words: "For long, long years!"

♣ ♣ ♣

EPILOGUE

BOSTON HARBOUR 4th OF JULY
200 YEARS LATER

The sun lights up the blue waters of the Massachusetts Bay. The fair summer day is so bright that it is hard to tell where the sky meets the sea.

A big crowd gathered on the shore, all look excited.

"And so your great-great-great-grand father John Dickenson married your great-great-great-grand mother Marie in fall of 1812. They had a long happy life together and died hours apart." A middle-aged man was saying to the boy of about seven, finishing his tale. "If not for the Constitution, neither you nor I would have been born."

"Daddy, how many kids they had?"

"John and Marie had three daughters and two sons. They named their sons Caleb and Isaac to honor Caleb Smith and the Constitution's Captain Isaac Hull."

"Daddy, did John buy the boat?" asks the boy.

"He sure did. And he built a new house."

"Did John go whaling?"

"My mother told me he was a fisherman afterwards."

"Did the British press our sailors when the War ended?"

"Not that I heard. They would not dare! The Constitution would not let them!" The man points at a single high white cloud coming towards them. "Oh, look, there she is!"

"Ready for a pony-ride? Here you are!" The man lifts his son and seats the boy onto his neck. "Can you see her?"

"I see sails! Many!" shouts the boy in delight.

"Right, that tall ship – taller than all the others - is the Constitution. Look, she sails unassisted, all sails set!"

"Daddy, what's that boom?" asks the boy, startled.

"She is firing her carronades in salute to the 4th of July! Huzzah, the Constitution!"

"Huzzah, the Constitution!" The thin boy's voice joins the crowd's cheering.

"She was there at the beginning of our nation!" ripples through the crowd.

"She fought for our freedom!"

"Look, she is escorted by the frigate USS 'Halyburton'!" A young man shouts in excitement, his camera clicking.

"And the destroyer USS 'Ramage'!" Another man echoes.

"She is taller than all modern ships!" A woman says, deeply amazed.

"Sure, her main mast is over a hundred seventy feet high!" The woman's husband clarifies.

Trying not to miss even a small detail, the crowd is watching as the Navy's 'Blue Angels' pass over the two hundred year-old ship's top-gallant sail and an American ensign flying proudly from the old frigate's main mast top.

Some people smile, others wipe tears as the Constitution is on her way, wind in her sails, smoke and great roar of her carronades the same as it was during her many battles.

Never defeated, she celebrated many victories:

1812 August 19	HMS Guerriere
1812 December 29	HMS Java
1815 February 20	HMS Cyane and
	HMS Levant

The Old Ironsides is priceless. Our ancestors kept her for us despite the scarce money the young country had a hundred fifty years ago.

Years will pass, still, like a first love, the frigate Constitution would never be forgotten by a Yankee heart.

Just a handful of the wooden ships 200 years of age still exist in the whole world. The Constitution is one of them!

Take your chance. Go to Boston to see her. Touch the ship's woodwork and feel her heart's beat. Let your kids feel as proud as the one who fought for the American freedom.

ENDNOTES

CHAPTER 1
James Frances' story is based on James Forten's biography:

> Privateers and Mariners in the Revolutionary War 01/12/2011
> http://www.usmm.org/revolution.html

CHAPTER 2
It is known that the Guerriere had ten American sailors in her crew: "Ten kidnapped Americans were among her crew" -

> John R. Spears. The History of our Navy from its origin to the present day, 1775 – 1897. Vol.2 1899 (New York Charles Scribner's sons)

However, I was not able to find their names. So, I used the name John Dickenson of the young man who was pressed by the British despite his Seaman Protection Certificate that he bought in 1809:

> * Ruth Dixon. Index to Semen's Protection Certificate Applications. Port of Philadelphia. 1995 (Baltimore, MD. Clearfield Co.)

> * A list Of Impressments from American Vessels into The British Service. American State Papers. Class I. Foreign Relation. Vol. III

CHAPTER 3
Captain Hull's orders from the Admiralty:

Gilbert Auchinleck. History of the war between Great Britain and the United States of America During the years 1812,1813, And 1814. 1855 (Toronto. Maclear and Co). p. 70

Captain Hull's family. Lt. Joseph Hull:

George Derby and James Terry White. The National Cyclopedia of American Biography. Being the History of the United States. 1906. (New York. James T. White &Co)

CHAPTER 4
Captain's and the crew's uniform description:

* Uniform Regulations, 1802. The Uniform Dress of the Captains and Certain Other Officers of the Navy of the United States. 1/12/2012 http://www.history.navy.mil/faqs/faq59-25.htm

* William Brady. Kedge-Anchor; or; Young Sailors' Assistant. 1863. (New York. London: Sampson, Low, Son & Co. Ludgate Hill).

CHAPTER 5

The way seamen talk is based on:

Herman Melville. Moby-Dick or The Whale. 1851.(New York. Harper & Brothers)

The powder boy Peter Furnace actually served on the Frigate Constitution:

Department of The Navy – Naval History And Heritage Command. Naval Historical Center Publication. The Constitution Gun Deck. 1/2/2011 http://www.history.navy.mil/library/online/con situtiongundeck.htm

The Surgeon's and the officers' names are real. The seamen' names with the exception of James Frances, Squeaking John, Ivan Stone and Old Jack are real too. They can be found in:

* The Analectic Magazine. Vol.1 1813 (H. Thomas. Philadelphia); p. 510

* Weekly Register; Documents, Essays, and Facts. From September 1812, to March 1813. Vol. III (H. Niles. Baltimore. The Franklin Press) p.28

CHAPTER 6
Navy Rations and small stores for 200 men for 4 months:

William Brady. Kedge-Anchor; or; Young Sailors' Assistant. 1863. (New York. London: Sampson, Low, Son & Co. Ludgate Hill) p 304-305

Ann Hart's story:

* **Bruce Grant**. Isaac Hull, Captain of Old Ironsides: The life and fighting times of Isaac Hull and the U.S. frigate Constitution. 1947. (Pellegrini and Cudahy) p.59

* The Constitution Museum. Hair Comb belonging to Ann Hull
12/8/11
http://www.ussconstitutionmuseum.org/proddi r/prod/496/18

Ann Hart's and Isaac Hull's portraits:

Looking Back: You've gotta have heart – Hart that is...
02/28/2012
http://www.shorelinetimes.com/articles/2012/0 2/09/opinion/doc4f340ef565682840135045.txt

The Constitution's decks, masts, sails, gulley-stove, etc.:

*

3/4/2012http://www.navy.mil/navydata/fact_di splay.asp?cid=4200&tid=100&ct=4

* Karl Heinz Marquardt. The 44-Gun Frigate USS Constitution, "Old Ironsides" (Anatomy of the Ship). 2005 (Publisher: Naval Institute Press)

CHAPTER 7
Commands "All hands 'bout the ship", etc.

John Harland. Seamanship in the age of sail. 1984.(Naval Institute Press)

CHAPTER 8
Carronades and long guns:

Department Of The Navy – Naval History And Heritage Command. Naval Historical Center Publication. The Constitution Gun Deck. 1/2/2011 http://www.history.navy.mil/library/online/con situtiongundeck.htm

CHAPTER 9
Squeaking John's story is based on:

George Derby and James Terry White. The National Cyclopedia of American Biography. Being the History of the United States. 1906. (New York. James T. White &Co)

CHAPTER 10
A piece of salted meat story is based on:

Richard Henry Dana, Jr. Two Years Before the Mast. 1869. (Boston. Fields, Osgood & Co).

CHAPTER 11
Santa Margareta's story:

James Fenimore Cooper. Old Ironsides. 1853.

CHAPTERS 12-16

The British Squadron's chaise of the Constitution near NJ coast:

* Captain Hull's official letters to the Admiralty;

* James Fenimore Cooper. Old Ironsides. 1853.;

* James Fenimore Cooper. History of the navy of the United States of America 1847. (Cooperstown. H.&E. Phivney);

* The Analectic Magazine. Vol.1 1813 (H. Thomas. Philadelphia);

* Weekly Register; Documents, Essays, and Facts. From September 1812, to March 1813. Vol. III (H. Niles. Baltimore. The Franklin Press) p.28

Lt. Morris expressing a lack of confidence in the Constitution sailing qualities:

> Ira N. Hollis.
> Cambridge, September 19, 1900. The frigate Constitution: the central figure of the Navy under sail. 1/13/2011
> http://www.archive.org/stream/frigateconstit ut00holl/frigateconstitut00holl_djvu.txt

p. 150

Poem "The Rime Of The Ancient Mariner":

Samuel Taylor Coleridge. The Rime Of The
Ancient Mariner. 1906 (Boston. Educational
Publishing Company).

CHAPTER 17

"Nothing was expected of the Navy.
Many merchant-ships were shut up in Boston, and
trade was dead. The open talk of secession and
the dismal prediction of disaster served only to
intensify the gloom." :

Ira N. Hollis.
Cambridge, September 19, 1900. The frigate
Constitution: the central figure of the Navy
under sail. 1/13/2011
http://www.archive.org/stream/frigateconstit
ut00holl/frigateconstitut00holl_djvu.txt

CHAPTER 18

Jack tar Asa Curtis reads the last issue of "Niles
Weekly Register":

Weekly Register; Documents, Essays, and
Facts. From September 1812, to March 1813.
Vol. II (H. Niles. Baltimore. The Franklin
Press) p.381

CHAPTERS 19-22

Are based on Captain Hull's official letters to the Admiralty and the work of the many authors as:

* James Fenimore Cooper. Old Ironsides. 1853.;

    * Tyrone G. Martin A Most Fortunate Ship. A Narrative History Of Old Ironsides. 1997 (Naval Institute Press. Annapolis, Maryland);

        -Midshipman Gilliam's the Guerriere's deck description:
        "...pieces of skulls, brains, legs, arms and blood...in every direction. ...Groans of the wounded were almost enough to make me curse the war" p.159

* Ira N. Hollis.
Cambridge, September 19, 1900. The frigate Constitution: the central figure of the Navy under sail 1/13/2011
http://www.archive.org/stream/frigateconstit ut00holl/frigateconstitut00holl_djvu.txt

    - "Just a bunch of convicts": p.165-168;

    - Alijah Adams' story: p. 166-167;

- Dacres's bible and long lasting friendship with I. Hull: p. 166;

- Captain Orne's story including the Guerriere's decks description. The drunken crew: p.168-170;

- Seaman Hogan re-attaching the fallen flag p. 170;

- "Dacres, give me your hand, I know you are hurt." p. 171;

- "Damn it. Jack, but we have made a brig of her!" p. 160;

* John R. Spears. The History of our Navy from its origin to the present day, 1775 – 1897. Vol.2 1899 (New York Charles Scribner's sons)

- "Ten kidnapped Americans were among her crew but the humane Dacres had not compelled them to fight against their own flag";

- Gold Medal for Hull and $50,000 for the crew: p. 94;

-"No, I will not take a sword from the one who..." p. 94

-"Now, boys, hull her" p. 83;

-"Hurrah, my boys! We've made a brig of her!" p.84
-"There is a Yankee frigate, in 45 min she is ours..." p.76;
- "A bunch of pine boards" p. 73

CHAPTER 21

How the Constitution was built:

* Thomas C. Gillmer "Old Ironsides. The rise, decline and restoration of the USS Constitution" 1993. (International Marine. Camden, Maine.);

* David Weitzman "Old Ironsides. Americans Build a Fighting Ship" 1996 (Houghton Miffin Company. Boston)

CHAPTER 22

The list of wounded and killed:

The Analectic Magazine. Vol.1 1813 (H. Thomas. Philadelphia); p. 510

CHAPTER 26

Ira N. Hollis.
Cambridge, September 19, 1900. The frigate Constitution: the central figure of the Navy under sail. 1/13/2011

Never Defeated: The Frigate Constitution

http://www.archive.org/stream/frigateconstitut
00holl/frigateconstitut00holl_djvu.txt

- "Their newspapers and even their
naval historian, James, could not find words
vile enough to describe us, and reference to
our frigates as " manned by a handful of
bastards and outlaws " p. 174;

- "A seaman on the Constitution, John
Cheever by name, was lying desperately
wounded by the side of a dead comrade.
When he heard the words, 'The enemy has
struck!' he raised himself on one hand, gave
three cheers, and fell back dead." p.186;

- Philip Freneau's poem:

Burton Egbert Stevenson. Poems of
American History. 1908. (Boston and
New York. Houghton Mifflin Company)

- New York City Mayor DeWitt
Clinton's speech:

James G. Wilson. The Memorial History
of the City of New-York. From its first
settlement to the year 1892. Vol. III.
1893 (New-York History Company)
p.247.

CHAPTER 27

"Next to impossible":

200-year old Portsmouth Yard began with one
Hull of a leader. Isaac Hull Comes to
Portsmouth Yard.
2/3/2011
http://www.seacoastnh.com/navyyard/isaachul
l.html#top

Oliver Wendell Holmes' poem "Old Ironsides":

2/28/2012
http://en.wikipedia.org/wiki/Old_Ironsides_(po
em)

CPSIA information can be obtained at www.ICGtesting.com
Printed in the USA
BVOW011718220312

285698BV00001B/5/P